A dangerous game

"What's going on?" Faith cried.

"Yeah," Rachel moaned. "Where are we?"

I took a deep breath. "I'm not sure," I said. "But I think that maybe we're . . ."

Before I could finish, something moved behind the trees in front of us. Something big. Faith's eyes popped and her mouth opened in horror.

I looked up, but even before I saw anything, I knew what it was. Something big and scaly—make that *huge* and scaly. And it was coming toward us fast!

CYBER ZONE™

Lost in Dino World

S. F. Black

Art direction by Fabia Wargin.
Cover art by Broeck Steadman.

Printed in the United States of America.

10 9 8 7 6 5 4 3 2 1

Chapter 1

"Check this one out," Faith said. "It's totally me!"

My best friend, Faith, and I were looking at stuff in Fossils, this weird secondhand store in our town. The small shop sold an amazing collection of junk—antique furniture, old china, and old clothes. But the store had obviously been named for its great fossil collection.

My dad, who's a paleontologist (fossil expert, in English) at the college in our town, said the number of fossils the dusty little store had for sale was surprising. He often went there to browse, hoping to discover a bone from an unknown dinosaur. But my mom, who's a paleontologist, too, never did.

She said Fossils was so dark and dingy and crammed with junk it gave her the creeps.

I had to agree. But I needed to get my dad something for his birthday, and his favorite present is—you guessed it—fossils! Plus, our school was having a Halloween dance the following Friday. This morning Faith had seen some extra-cool costumes in the shop window, so she'd come along with me.

Faith held up the dress she'd just pulled down from the rack. "So, what do you think?" she demanded. "Is it perfect, or what?"

"It's neat," I said, hardly glancing over. I was thinking about getting my dad one of the trilobite fossils on the table by the door. Trilobites may sound like some sort of amazing creature, but they're really just shells—kind of like prehistoric hermit crabs. I sighed. A trilobite fossil was a great present for someone who didn't know much about prehistoric life. But for a paleontologist, it would be pretty boring.

Faith's voice broke in on my thoughts. "Brooke! You weren't even looking." She waved the dress under my nose. "Come on, don't you think it's totally awesome?"

I blinked. The dress definitely was cool. It was a 1920s-style beaded evening gown with a wild snakeskin pattern. That was another weird thing about Fossils. Almost all the junk in it had something to do with reptiles—snakes, lizards, and, of course, dinosaurs.

"You're right. It's amazing," I said, smiling.

Faith added it to the stack of dresses she was already holding. "Come on." She tugged at my arm. "You've got to come with me while I try these on." She pulled me toward the front of the store.

We walked up to the counter, and Faith asked Mrs. Trowdon, the owner of Fossils, if there was somewhere she could try on the dresses.

Mrs. Trowdon just shrugged and rasped, "I suppose." She came out from behind the counter and walked to the back of the store.

Mrs. Trowdon was majorly weird. She always wore heavy shawls and scarves and hats—even in the summer. She hardly ever spoke to customers.

"I guess that means 'yes,'" Faith whispered with a nervous giggle as we followed Mrs. Trowdon to a door near the back entrance. She opened the door, eyed the two of us suspiciously, and then shuffled back to the front counter.

The dressing room turned out to be a kind of closet. A huge wardrobe was shoved against the back wall, and it was stuffed with junk. Boy, was it ever dusty in there. It was all I could do to keep from sneezing. I'm not a big fan of dust. I'm more the neat-freak type—tidy and organized.

"Yech!" I said, wrinkling up my nose.

"Just tell me what you think of this dress," Faith commanded, ignoring the clutter around us.

She pulled the snakeskin dress over her head. "How does it look?" she asked as she did a little turn.

"It looks terrific," I replied.

It was true. Faith looked really pretty in the dress. But then, Faith *is* really pretty. She has long, curly red hair and green eyes. She also has tons of freckles, which she hates. But even freckles look good on her.

I'm not ugly, but compared with Faith, I am pretty ordinary looking. For one thing, I'm skinny. For another, I'm not very tall. I have long, straight, dark brown hair and no freckles or distinguishing marks.

The only unusual thing about me is my eyes. They're big and light brown, very light brown. In fact, some people, whom I prefer not to name, have claimed my eyes are yellow. My mom says they're amber, which sounds a lot better. Still, they are kind of a strange color, and not a good strange, either.

Faith eyed her reflection in the cracked mirror behind the door. "Will Mark Harris think I look good in this?" she asked.

I rolled my eyes. Maybe because she's so pretty, Faith is also the most boy-crazy girl in the sixth grade.

"Who cares what Mark Harris thinks?" I mumbled.

"I do!" Faith answered.

Mark Harris is a real jock. A lot of girls in our class are crazy about him. Not me. I think he's brain-dead. I've tried to talk to Mark a couple of times, but all he cares about is sports.

I shrugged. "Well, he'll probably like it," I told her honestly. Then I frowned. I wasn't here to talk about clothes with Faith; I was here to find a great birthday present for my dad.

"Maybe I should just get him a trilobite," I murmured. "But that's so boring."

Faith had taken off the snakeskin dress and was pulling on another one. It was made of shiny red material, with big triangular spikes down the arms and back.

"What about this one?" she asked.

"It looks great, too," I said enthusiastically. The dress looked sort of like a dinosaur costume, which made me happy, because I love dinosaurs.

Faith frowned at her reflection. "Are you sure it doesn't make me look like a brontosaurus or something?"

"A brontosaurus?" I repeated.

"Yeah. You know, because of the spiky back."

I sighed loudly. "Faith! *Brontosaurus* isn't the right word. You mean *apatosaurus*. And *Apatosaurus* doesn't have a spiky back—*Stegosaurus* does!"

"Oh," Faith mumbled. "Well, you know what I mean."

I sighed again. No matter how many times I've tried to teach Faith the correct names for different dinosaurs, she always forgets which is which. Faith thinks dinosaurs are majorly boring. It's amazing we're best friends. My mom says the fact that we are proves that opposites attract.

Faith loves clothes and boys and hates school—especially science. I could care less about clothes or boys. I like school okay, and I love science. Plus, I'm crazy about dinosaurs. I know it may seem strange for a twelve-year-old girl to prefer dinosaurs to boys, but I definitely do.

I sighed again and wished for the millionth time that Faith could take a little more interest in my life's passion. But I knew Faith would never share my love of dinosaurs.

"Who cares about some big, dumb creatures that lived trillions of years ago?" she said to me once. And she stuck by her opinion, even when I explained that dinosaurs died out only sixty-five million years ago, and not all of them were big and dumb—some dinosaurs were actually fast moving and highly intelligent.

None of my other friends are into dinosaurs, either. In fact, I know only one kid who is as interested in them as I am: Billy Zipkin.

Billy is a boy in my class. He knows a ton about dinosaurs. Unfortunately, he's also obnoxious. He's always doing stuff like sticking spiders in girls' desks and laughing like an idiot when they get scared. Billy thinks all girls are dumb. Even though we're both dino freaks, there's no way I would ever be friends with Billy Zipkin.

But then I cheered up. Although everyone at school (except awful Billy) could care less about dinosaurs, I now knew other people who shared my passion. My parents had bought me a computer last month. They'd also paid for an Internet connection. Two weeks before our Fossils shopping trip, I had discovered a totally cool chat room: Dino World. The kids on Dino World were as crazy about dinosaurs as I was. Some knew even more about dinosaurs than me—especially one kid who called himself Lizard Boy.

I gazed in the mirror and blushed. I would never admit it to Faith, but if Lizard Boy went to my school, I'd probably have a crush on him, just like Faith has on Mark Harris. At least, if he wasn't totally hideous or something.

Faith pulled off the red dress and put the snakeskin one back on. "Here," she said, tossing the red dress at me. "Why don't you try this one on? It would be perfect for you."

"You mean you want me to look like a stegosaur?" I joked.

Faith wrinkled her nose. "Brooke! Of course not! It's just that the red will really bring out the color of your hair."

"You mean it'll bring out my dull brown?" I mumbled.

Faith sighed. "Brooke, stop it. Don't you want to get a great dress to wear to the dance?"

"Not really," I said. I didn't even know if I wanted to go to the dance. "What I want is to find a present for my dad."

"Brooke, just try it on. Please?"

"Okay, okay," I said. I bent down to untie my shoes. But as I stood up, I slammed right into the big old wardrobe. "Ouch!" I yelped. Then I gasped. Something had fallen on top of me.

Faith screamed.

I reached up to move the object aside. Then I screamed, too. A pair of giant claws was digging into my skin!

Chapter 2

"It's alive!" Faith wailed.

I pushed the giant claws off me. My heart felt like it was beating triple time. I turned to look at whatever was back there.

"No, it's not," I cried, peering at the huge, clawed creature looming over me. "It's stuffed. It's just a model or something. It looks like some kind of dinosaur."

I squinted at the weird-looking stuffed creature. It was big, but small for a dinosaur. Then I recognized it: *Coelophysis. Coelophysis* was sometimes called the wolf of the dinosaur world. In a way, it was a lot like a wolf. It weighed about sixty-five pounds and probably hunted in packs. It also moved fast and may have been warm-blooded.

I looked at the model beside me and shivered. Sixty-five pounds wasn't that big. But some scientists thought *Coelophysis* was about the most ferocious small dinosaur that ever existed. And this model was very realistic. In fact, it was the greatest dinosaur model I'd ever seen. Its glass eyes gleamed brightly, and its mouth was twisted in a horrible grimace. The thing looked almost alive! And there was something else about it—something strange . . .

Before I finished my thought, the door to the closet sprang open.

"What's going on in here?" Mrs. Trowdon hissed.

I stepped forward.

"Nothing, ma'am," I stammered. "I just bumped into the wardrobe and knocked this, uh . . . dinosaur model down onto myself. It scared my friend and me, that's all."

I glanced over at Faith. She still looked scared. In fact, she looked totally terrified!

"No big deal," I added, trying to sound calm and relaxed. But my voice came out all high and squeaky.

I glanced over at the model again. Then I realized what made it so strange. Instead of being covered with scales, the model was covered in small, greenish feathers.

My heart leaped into my mouth. I'd never seen a model of a dinosaur covered in feathers before. Someone who didn't know anything about dinosaurs might think the feathers were just a dumb mistake. But I knew better. Over the past few years, scientists have started to think that some small meat-eating dinosaurs (such as *Coelophysis*) may have been covered with feathers instead of scales.

That's because scientists have decided that modern reptiles such as lizards and snakes aren't the only descendants of dinosaurs. Birds are, too. Everyone who studies dinosaurs is really excited about this idea. If it's true, it could mean that not all dinosaurs were cold-blooded, like today's reptiles are. Some might have been warm-blooded, like us. Those dinosaurs would have had the energy to move fast. They also might have been a lot smarter than we've ever imagined.

I touched one of the feathers. It felt prickly. "This

model is pretty unusual," I said aloud.

"It's old. Very old," Mrs. Trowdon whispered.

She stepped into the room. Her eyes gleamed strangely in the dim light. I'd never noticed before what color they were—a light yellow-brown, like mine. "Here, I'd better put it away," she said stiffly. "It's very valuable." She hoisted up the large model and stuck it back on top of the wardrobe.

I looked up at her. "The model's old?" I babbled. "That's weird, because it has feathers, and—"

I broke off. Something about the expression in Mrs. Trowdon's eyes stopped me from saying more. Her eyes narrowed, and she was staring at me the way a snake looks at a mouse. I shivered.

"Because what?" she rasped.

I swallowed. "Oh, nothing. Just that I've never seen a model of a dinosaur with feathers on it before."

"So," Mrs. Trowdon said abruptly, "have you girls finished trying on clothes?"

"Yes, we're all done, I guess," Faith stuttered.

"Do you want to buy any of these dresses?"

"Yeah, sure, I guess. I mean, I do," Faith answered. "How about you, Brooke? Do you want to buy the red dress?"

"No, I think I'll leave it," I said. I looked up at Mrs. Trowdon again. "But I'm definitely interested in the *Coelophysis* model. How much do you want for it?"

Mrs. Trowdon turned away without answering. "Well, get changed quickly! We're closing up soon," she growled. She took the snakeskin-patterned dress out of Faith's hands. "I'll take this up front for you."

"Th-thanks," Faith stuttered.

"But the model?" I called as Mrs. Trowdon shut the

closet door behind her. "How much do you want for the model?"

"Brooke, you could never afford to buy that," Faith whispered.

"Yeah, I know, but it's the perfect birthday present for my dad," I hissed back. "If I ask Mrs. Trowdon to hold it, maybe my mom would help me pay for it."

"I bet it costs a fortune," Faith said.

"Yeah, but my dad would totally love it," I replied.

We changed into our own clothes and went to the front of the store. Mrs. Trowdon was standing behind the cash register.

"I think ten dollars for this dress would be fair, don't you?" she muttered to Faith as we came up.

Faith smiled. "Yeah, sounds great." Then she whispered in my ear, "I can see why some people like this store. It's dirt cheap."

I cleared my throat. "I was thinking about buying the model of *Coelophysis* you have in the closet," I said. "How much is it?"

"It's not for sale," a voice croaked behind me.

I whirled around. A boy was standing there. He looked about my age. But it was hard to see his face because he was wearing a black baseball cap pulled down low over his eyes.

"That's too bad," I replied. "My dad would love it. He teaches paleontology at the college," I explained. "He comes in here a lot to buy fossils."

Neither Mrs. Trowdon nor the boy said anything.

I squinted at the boy. Even with the cap pulled over his face, I could see he looked a lot like Mrs. Trowdon. He had the same dark hair, pale skin, and narrow, pointy face. I decided he must be her son.

14

On the way to the shop, Faith had told me Mrs. Trowdon had a son who was our age but didn't go to our school. Even though he was supposed to be in boarding school someplace, Faith had seen him around a lot lately. Just that past week, she'd seen a bunch of kids teasing him. "They were following him down the street, calling him 'reptile,'" she'd said.

"Why *reptile*?" I'd asked.

Faith had shrugged. "I guess because he and his mom look sort of like reptiles," she'd replied.

I could see what Faith meant. He *did* look sort of snakelike. I wondered where the Trowdons were from. Were they Scottish or Irish or Russian or something? Their name sounded sort of familiar to me. Maybe I'd met someone with the same name before, but I couldn't think where.

"Are you sure you won't sell the model?" I asked.

"I said 'no,' didn't I?" the boy growled.

"I see." I was beginning to get angry. "Well, if you change your mind, let me know, because I'd be very interested in buying it. I'll just leave my name and number and—"

"Don't bother," the boy cut in. "I told you, we're not selling. So why don't you just pay for your stuff and go?" He turned and stalked to the back of the store.

I stared after him, my cheeks burning. I couldn't believe how rude he was. I also couldn't believe Mrs. Trowdon wasn't telling her son to be more polite to her customers.

"Here's your change," Mrs. Trowdon said flatly. She pushed some bills across the counter at us. "You'd better go now. We're about to close," she went on coldly. She nodded at us both. "Have a nice day," she added, without a trace of a smile, as we shuffled out.

As soon as we stepped into the street, the door slammed shut behind us. I whirled around. The CLOSED sign was already hanging in the door, and a dusty shade had been pulled down over the window.

Chapter 3

"Talk about strange!" Faith breathed. She glanced back at the closed storefront and shivered slightly.

"Yeah," I agreed. "They weren't exactly friendly."

"*Rude* is the word I'd use." Faith tossed her long red hair over her shoulders. "I can't believe they treat their customers that way. No wonder they don't get much business!"

"*Uh-huh,*" I murmured absentmindedly.

I was still thinking about the model of *Coelophysis*. I'd never seen such a lifelike model of a dinosaur before—not even when Dad and Mom had taken me to the Smithsonian in Washington, D.C. And the Smithsonian has the best dinosaur re-creations in the whole country. I was also wondering why the model had feathers. That wasn't surprising, since the theory about birds being descended from dinosaurs is fairly new. What *was* surprising was that it looked so convincing. I would have expected a model of a dinosaur with feathers to look bizarre. But this one didn't. It looked almost real.

But what was really puzzling was Mrs. Trowdon's saying that the model was very old. The back of my neck started to prickle. There was definitely something odd about all this.

"I'll have to ask the kids on Dino World about it," I muttered aloud.

Faith shot me a look. In the dim twilight, her green eyes shone like a cat's. "You're still thinking about that yucky stuffed dinosaur, aren't you?" she asked.

I shrugged. "Sort of."

"So what's the big deal about it?"

I shrugged again. "Nothing, really."

"Brooke!" Faith's eyes flashed. "We've only been best friends since second grade, remember? I can tell when something is up with you. And something is definitely up! So spill the beans already!"

I bit my lip. "It's just that the model is weird."

"Of course it's weird," Faith joked. "All dinosaurs are weird." Then her face became serious. "'Weird' how?"

"Didn't you notice that it has feathers?"

"Yeah. So?"

"Well, some paleontologists have only recently hypothesized—"

"Hy-potha-what?" Faith squawked. "Please, Brooke, say it in plain English, okay?"

"They guessed only recently that some dinosaurs might have had feathers."

"So?" Faith said again.

I sighed. This was going to be hard to explain. "Well, Mrs. Trowdon said the model is very old. But it can't be, because the idea that some dinosaurs might have had feathers is a new one."

Faith finished for me. "So if it's old, how would the person who made the model have known to put feathers on it?"

I grinned. Faith can sometimes be a lot quicker than I expect her to be. "Right!" I said. "But there's probably some reasonable explanation. Like maybe Mrs. Trowdon lied."

Faith shook her head. "I don't think so. She didn't sound like she was lying. And she didn't start acting abrupt until you pointed out that the model had feathers." Faith wrinkled her forehead. "There's definitely a mystery here," she declared. "The question is, what are we going to do about it?"

"Do about it?" I gaped at her. "What are you talking about? We're not going to do *anything* about it!"

"But Brooke, we have to do something!" Faith's eyes were glowing with excitement. I sighed softly. I knew that look. It meant Faith had an idea. When Faith got ideas, you had to watch out.

"Like what sort of something?" I asked warily.

"Well, you said you were going to ask the kids on Dino World about it. So I'll come over to your house, and we'll both ask them. At least that's a good place to start."

"To start what?"

Faith lowered her voice. "Solving the mystery."

"But there isn't any mystery," I protested. "It's just kind of odd, that's all."

"Omigosh," Faith shrieked, grabbing my arm. "Maybe it's not a model of a coel-whatever-it-is. Maybe it's a real stuffed one!"

I sighed. "Faith, that's impossible," I explained. "Dinosaurs have been extinct for sixty-five million years. There's no way a stuffed coelophysis could be just hanging around in some old, run-down shop."

Faith stuck out her lower lip. "Brooke, nothing is impossible," she informed me grandly. "Maybe the coel-whatever-he's-called got mummified in an Arctic snowstorm or something."

"Faith, they didn't have Arctic snowstorms at the time

of the dinosaurs," I cut in. "Look, it's not a real stuffed coelophysis, all right? It's just sort of peculiar, that's all. Anyhow," I finished lamely, "I have a feeling that model is just another one of life's little mysteries that will never be solved."

"Unless we solve it," Faith retorted. "Like I said, we'll go to your house. I'll call my mom and tell her I'm spending the night. Then we'll both check out that dino talk place. Maybe some of those dino nuts will be able to give us some great clues!"

"What are you, some kind of genius detective?" I burst out.

"Yup," Faith nodded happily. "Why not? I've always wanted to be Harriet the Spy."

"Harriet the Spy isn't a detective," I shot back.

"Close enough," said Faith. "Anyway, I think it would be cool to be a detective, don't you?"

"Not really," I muttered. "I just want to be a paleontologist."

"That's why we're the perfect team to solve this mystery," Faith said. "It's got dinosaurs and everything!"

She slung the plastic bag holding her dress for the dance over her shoulder and took off down the street. I sprinted to catch up. "But what if my mom doesn't want you to spend the night?" I asked.

"She will," Faith replied confidently. "It's Friday, remember? And your mom and dad love me." It was true. Mom and Dad did love Faith. They thought having such a lively, bubbly best friend was great for me. I think they worried that I'd do nothing but study all the time if Faith wasn't around.

"All right, you win," I said. "But let me do the talking on Dino World, okay?"

Faith grinned. "No prob." Then she slapped me on the back. "Chill out, Brooke," she said. "Solving this mystery is going to be our greatest adventure ever!"

I looked up and down the shadowy street. My teeth started to chatter, and I didn't know why. But Faith's words gave me the feeling we were headed for big trouble.

Chapter 4

"Okay, let's get going," Faith commanded.

I stared at her. I couldn't believe Faith was so eager to log on to the Internet. She's usually even less interested in computers than she is in dinosaurs.

But not tonight. She'd gotten permission from her parents to spend the night. My parents had agreed, too. And now we were sitting in front of my computer desk. I switched on my computer and my modem.

"Pass the chips and dip," Faith said. "If I'm going to talk to a bunch of A-student dino nuts, I'm going to need some serious brain food."

"You could be an A student if you ever opened a book," I told her, handing over the bowl of chips.

"Yeah, only I don't happen to have a photographic memory, like yours!" Faith retorted. She took an extra-large chip and dunked it in my special onion dip.

"Having a good memory doesn't make you any smarter, Faith."

"Maybe not," she replied, "but it's a real help when it comes to history tests, Miss Perfect."

I blushed. I always get A's on history tests. My memory helps. But that's not the only reason I do well in school—not that I can ever make Faith believe that. She thinks having a photographic memory makes school a snap for me. Honest, it doesn't. All it means is that, if I concentrate really hard, I can re-create a picture of something I've seen, like a page in a textbook.

The truth is, if I try very, very hard, I can make a picture so real I can actually see it in my head. Not all people with photographic memories can do that.

When I was a little kid, I used to imagine putting animal heads on people around me. I used to give my kindergarten teacher, Mrs. Murray, a monkey's head and Mr. Bowdon, our elementary-school principal, the head of a donkey.

Mom says I'll appreciate having a photographic memory when I'm older. She says she knows, because she has one too. Mom says we inherited this special trait from her grandmother. I never met my great-grandmother, but she made a big impression on my mom. Whenever she talks about her grandmother, Mom gets this weird, dreamy look on her face. "I wish you could have met her, Brooke," she always says. "She was an incredible woman."

I always wonder if Mom says that because my great-grandmother had a photographic memory or because of something else about her. But whenever I ask, Mom changes the subject. If I say, "Why was she so incredible?" Mom replies, "She just was, that's all." That doesn't give a person much to go on.

I guess having a photographic memory is sort of cool, but I've often wished I had red hair or green eyes instead. It's not much fun when the most amazing thing about you is something no one can see.

I sighed and started to log on to the Internet. Beside me, Faith dunked another chip in dip and crunched loudly. Then she leaned forward, watching the screen eagerly. "What's going on?" she whispered.

"Nothing," I replied. "I'm just logging on." I typed in my on-line name, *DinoGirl,* and went to the Internet directory. I scrolled until I came to the on-line address of my favorite chat room. I clicked my mouse. Faith shuddered as an image of a ferocious-looking tyrannosaur appeared on the screen. It was the home page for Dino World.

"Yech! Talk about ugly," she murmured. "Brooke, how can you like those monsters?"

"Look, I just do," I replied. "Are you going to do this with me or not?"

"Sure," Faith said quickly. "I may not like dinosaurs, but I love mysteries. And I definitely want to solve this one."

I groaned quietly. In the first place, I wasn't sure there was a mystery to be solved. In the second place, I felt nervous about going into the Dino World chat room with Faith. She'd promised to let me do all the talking. But I know Faith, and I knew that at some point she'd want to put in her two cents. I almost hoped Lizard Boy wouldn't be there tonight.

Then I felt ashamed of myself. Faith might not know much about dinosaurs, but she's my best friend and a great person. I clicked my mouse again, and the chat room screen appeared.

Hello, it's Dino Girl. Anyone there? I typed in.

A ribbon of letters appeared. *Hey, Dino Girl. Zippy here.*

Zippy is a regular on Dino World. He's sort of a jerk in my opinion, but he knows a lot about dinosaurs. *Tonight's topic is "dino moms." Anything you want to add to the discussion, Dino Girl?*

Actually, no, I typed back. *Today I'm more interested in talking about* Coelophysis.

Immediately a new ribbon of letters appeared on the screen. *What do you want to know about* Coelophysis?— *Lizard Boy.*

The moment I saw the words *Lizard Boy,* my heart started to beat faster. Pretty dumb, huh? I mean, how can you have a crush on some kid you've never met?

Hi, Lizard Boy! I typed rapidly. *Good to hear from you. How's it been going?*

"Hey," Faith said with a frown, "why are you getting all personal all of a sudden? We're here to get information, remember?"

"Of course I remember," I replied stiffly. "It's just that he's sort of a pal of mine."

"You mean, you know him?" Faith asked.

"No, of course not. He's just an on-line pal," I explained quickly. "We've talked a lot on Dino World. Lizard Boy knows an incredible amount about dinosaurs. In fact, he's the perfect person to help us."

"I see." A wicked grin crept across Faith's face. "You know, Brooke, if I didn't know that you have no interest in boys, I'd say you like this lizard guy."

"No way!" I said hotly. "Anyway, how could I like someone I've never even met?"

"It's been known to happen," Faith replied mysteriously.

I ignored her. Instead I typed, *Lizard Boy, I want to learn everything I can about* Coelophysis. *Can you help?* I waited for Lizard Boy to come back at me with a flood of information the way he usually did. But instead, Zippy answered for him: Coelophysis *was a puny meat-eating dinosaur that lived in the late Triassic period.*

"What's the Triassic period?" Faith demanded.

"The Triassic period is the earliest time that dinosaurs lived on Earth," I replied. "It started about 245 million years ago."

"Wow! You mean that thing we saw was 245 million years old?" Faith demanded.

"No, of course not! I told you, it's just a model," I replied. *The late Triassic?* I typed in. *Are you sure?*

Positive, Zippy replied.

I frowned.

"What's wrong?" Faith said.

"Nothing. I just forgot that *Coelophysis* lived that long ago," I said.

Faith shrugged. "Sixty-five million years, 245 million years—what's the difference?"

"You don't understand. Things were really different in the Triassic period," I told her.

"How different?"

"In the late Triassic, all the land on Earth was just one giant continent called Pangaea."

"I don't see how that changes anything," Faith sniffed.

"Well, it was always warm and sunny. There was no winter anywhere in the world. So if *Coelophysis* lived back then, it wouldn't have needed feathers."

Faith frowned. "I don't get it," she said.

"Look, scientists believe dinosaurs developed feathers to keep warm," I explained patiently. "And if it was always warm, they wouldn't have needed feathers. That's why most scientists think dinosaurs became birds much later, sometime in the Cretaceous period. The end of the Cretaceous was when the dinosaurs became extinct."

"Brooke, you're making my head spin," Faith groaned. "But I think I get your drift. So how do you explain that model in Fossils?"

I sighed. "It was probably just a mistake."

"Maybe," Faith said, unconvinced. "Anyway, it couldn't hurt to ask the dino nuts about it."

I had to admit she was right. I leaned over my keyboard again. *Thanks, Zippy,* I wrote. *How about feathers? Is there any chance* Coelophysis *had feathers?*

Feathers? Zippy shot back. *Use your brain, Dino Girl! We're talking about the Triassic period, remember?*

Zippy typed in a flame sign. People in chat rooms use them when they want to point out that you've just said something really dumb or when they want to insult you for some reason. Don't ask me why, but some people on the Internet love flaming one another.

Look, I replied, *I know as much about the Triassic period as you do, Zippy.*

Then what's this junk about feathers?

I was deciding how I should reply when Faith pushed me aside. *Look, Zip-moron,* she typed in, *Dino Girl rules when it comes to dinosaurs, okay? So just answer the question, and stop acting like a dumb boy!*

Way to go, Dino Girl, typed in someone who called herself Rachel.

I groaned and covered my eyes. Not only had Faith insulted Zippy, but everyone on Dino World thought *I'd* done it.

"Faith," I hissed, "I told you to let me do the talking."

"I know, but that Zippy guy was insulting you."

"That's just how Zippy is," I said. "We all try to ignore him. Now I won't be able to get any information out of him."

"Who needs his information?" Faith replied. "It's obvious that Zippy thinks he knows everything, but he doesn't."

She leaned over the computer again. I watched nervously as her fingers danced over the keys. *So is there a chance this dino had feathers or not?* Faith asked.

I told you, no way! Zippy wrote.

How can you be so sure?

Simple logic. If dinosaurs had feathers, they developed them much later, when they were in the process of evolving into birds, Zippy replied.

*But doesn't evol—*Faith's fingers paused. "Brooke, how do you spell evolution?"

"E-v-o-l-u-t-i-o-n."

—ution take millions, maybe billions of years? Faith wrote. *So how can you say for certain that this dino wasn't an early example of a feathered dinosaur?*

I glanced over at Faith in surprise. For someone who could care less about science or dinosaurs, she had asked a pretty smart question.

Zippy didn't answer for a moment. Then he typed, *You do have a point, but no one has ever found even one measly bit of evidence that* Coelophysis *had feathers.*

True, typed in Lizard Boy. *The real question is, why do you believe* Coelophysis *might have had feathers, Dino Girl?*

Faith looked at me. "What should I say?" she asked.

I frowned. "Let me answer," I said, pushing her aside. *Look,* Coelophysis *was pretty small for a meat-eating dinosaur, right? That's why it had to hunt in packs. Scientists can also tell from skeletons that* Coelophysis *could move really fast, way faster than any reptile around today. So how did* Coelophysis *maintain its body heat?*

Feathers would have helped it stay warm.

Good point, Dino Girl, Lizard Boy replied. *But if temperatures were always warm on Pangaea, maybe* Coelophysis *didn't need to work very hard to maintain its body heat.*

Yes, but—I hesitated a moment. *Scientists say* Coelophysis *might have done a lot of hunting at night. How did it stay warm then?*

All right, so Coelophysis *hunted at night,* Lizard Boy replied. *In fact, night was its favorite time to hunt.* Coelophysis *could see really well in the dark. But think about it, Dino Girl. Even if* Coelophysis *hunted at night, it*—

But before he could go on, Faith leaned over me and typed in quickly: *How do you know so much, Lizard Boy? Did you live there or something?*

Lizard Boy didn't reply.

I hid my head in my hands. "Faith!" I moaned. "What are you doing?" I couldn't believe she'd insulted my best on-line friend like that. "What's gotten into you?"

"Nothing," Faith said huffily. "It's just that he's even worse than Zippy. I mean, to hear him talk, you'd think he was personal friends with the dinosaurs."

I sighed deeply. "Look, he just knows a lot. After a while, you do sort of feel like you know the dinosaurs."

I leaned over my keyboard again. *Lizard Boy, are you there? Sorry, Lizard Boy, I wasn't trying to flame you, honest,* I wrote. *I guess I'm just really curious about this feather idea. Could* Coelophysis *have had feathers?*

It would appear very unlikely, Lizard Boy answered. I could tell he was still mad, because he doesn't usually talk that way. He sounds more like a regular kid—even if he does know more about dinosaurs than any other kid I've ever known.

Are you sure? I repeated lamely.

He said he was sure, didn't he? Zippy jumped in, adding another flame sign at the end.

It's a very interesting theory, though, Rachel typed politely.

It was girls against boys, just like at school.

Thanks, Rachel, I replied. *But I guess it's a wrong one.*

Faith's green eyes flashed. "Why do you say it's wrong?" she hissed softly.

"Lizard Boy and Zippy know a lot," I told her wearily. "If they say there's no way *Coelophysis* had feathers, they're probably right. The feathers on the model are probably just a mistake."

"I can't believe you're letting a bunch of boys tell you what to think," Faith shouted. She may be boy-crazy, but she doesn't let anyone push her around. "Maybe you should let me do some talking."

"Faith, please," I pleaded.

But Faith was already typing. *Zippy, Lizard Boy, you seem pretty sure you're right,* she wrote. *But what would you say if I said I'd seen a life-sized model of* Coelophysis *with feathers?*

You saw a model with feathers? Zippy typed back. *Weird!*

Where did you see this model? Lizard Boy asked.

Some junk store in town, Faith answered. *And the people who own the store acted totally strange about it.*

Strange how? piped up Rachel.

Yeah, what do you mean, strange? asked Zippy.

Faith had their interest now. I inched forward on my chair. I was waiting to see what Lizard Boy would say. If, somehow, we could find evidence that *Coelophysis* had had feathers, it would be a great discovery. I could just imagine the headlines: "Kid Dino-Lovers Overturn Theories of Dinosaur Life in the Triassic Period!" I knew something like that probably would never happen, but daydreaming about it was fun.

Where was this model? Zippy demanded.

Yeah, seconded Rachel. *I'd love to see it.*

The people who own it said it isn't for sale, Faith typed back

I'm sure someone with a brain could persuade them to sell it, Zippy wrote.

I rolled my eyes. It was a typical Zippy comment.

What for? Lizard Boy asked. *It's probably just a lame kid's toy. It can't be real.*

I secretly agreed with him. But I could tell Faith didn't. Somehow she'd gotten into her head that the model we'd seen was a real stuffed coelophysis. A tremor went up my spine. I had to admit that the thing had looked very realistic. But there was no way a little store like Fossils could have a real coelophysis skeleton lying around, let alone a preserved specimen. Skeletons of *Coelophysis* are rare, very rare. They'd been discovered in only one place in the whole world—New Mexico.

Anyway, Faith wrote, *the name of the store is—*

We don't need the name of the store, Lizard Boy cut in.

Why not? Zippy demanded.

Yeah, why not? Faith agreed. *The name of the store is—*

That's when it happened. My computer suddenly let out a horrible screeching noise. I jumped backward. So did Faith. Then we saw it. A huge ball of light, like an asteroid, came rushing out of my computer screen.

"Brooke," Faith gasped. "What's going on?"

Chapter 5

I tried to answer. I wanted to answer. But I couldn't. Something was happening to me—to us. Something unbelievable. Something terrifying!

At first, it felt like being caught in the glow of an incredibly bright spotlight. No matter how hard I blinked, all I could see was bright light all around me. Then I felt like I was being sucked up into the light, like I was moving faster and faster.

"Faith!" I tried to shout. But no sound came out of my mouth.

Now I was moving so fast, I felt like a lightning bolt. I stared around in disbelief. Miles ahead of me, I could see my feet, still in their red sneakers.

I tried to scream. But all I heard was a rushing sound, like the howl of the wind. Particles of light whizzed past me, and in them I thought I caught a glimpse of Faith's terrified face.

Then the world whirled even faster and everything went dark. The next thing I knew, I landed on a hard surface with a bone-crunching *thud*!

I opened my eyes, but the light around me was so bright that I had to shut them again. Instead, I tried to sit up. But that didn't work too well, either, because I felt as if I had just gotten off an extra-fast roller coaster. I shut my eyes tighter, afraid I was going to barf. The spinning slowed down. Then it stopped.

Now I could hear a strange buzzing that sounded like lots of insects. I let out a groan. Every bone in my body ached. I felt as if my arms and legs had been stretched like rubber bands and then snapped back into place. I cautiously opened one eye.

Honestly, I expected to see my room—my computer desk, my Smithsonian dinosaur poster, and my shiny brass bed.

But I didn't. Instead, I was looking up at a huge, cloudless blue sky. I blinked and sat up in a hurry.

Wherever I was, I was pretty sure I had never been there before. I was sitting on a big rock with funny-looking bushes and trees growing around it. The trees seemed too tall. And there was something odd about the sky. It was bigger and bluer than any sky I'd ever seen. The air felt warm and moist.

I glanced around wildly. Then I saw Faith lying on a rock behind me. Her eyes were closed, and I couldn't see her breathing. She looked dead.

"Faith! Faith!" I screamed.

She opened her eyes and sat up. "*Oww*, my head hurts," she moaned. "What happened, Brooke? Did your dumb computer electrocute us or something?" Her voice suddenly trailed off. "Hey!" she said. She opened her eyes wider. "Brooke, where are we?"

"I don't know," I replied in a tiny voice.

The trees above us looked sort of like pine trees. But they kind of looked like palm trees, too. They had huge branches that splayed out from tall trunks like palm fronds. I squinted at them. I knew I'd never seen any trees like them, but they looked familiar somehow. Then I heard something—the burbling sound of rapidly rushing water. I shaded my eyes. We were close to a wide river. The water shone clear and silvery in the sun.

I swallowed. I had never seen any place so beautiful. But there was something creepy about it, too.

"What is this place?" Faith whispered. "Do you think your computer could have sent us to Florida?"

"I don't think this is Florida," I replied solemnly.

"I hope it's not heaven," Faith murmured.

"I don't think it can be," I said. "I mean, I feel weird, but I don't feel dead."

"You're definitely not dead," a voice said behind us.

I whirled around. A girl I'd never seen before stood on the other side of the rock. She was short, with blond hair and thick glasses. I stared at her.

"Who are you?" I breathed.

"My name is Rachel," the girl replied. "I just took my pulse, and it's normal. I can't be dead, which means you can't be, either. My dad's a doctor, so I know about pulses and stuff," she added in a wavery voice.

"You're Rachel?" I cried. "From the chat room?"

Rachel's eyes widened. "You mean, you're from Dino World, too?" she demanded.

"Yup. I'm Dino Girl, but my real name is Brooke," I explained. My mind was racing. If Rachel was here, there was a good chance that all the kids from the chat room were here, including Lizard Boy. The question was how and why?

I glanced up at the weird-looking trees again. Suddenly I sucked in my breath. I knew why they looked so familiar. I *had* seen them before. At least, I'd seen pictures of them before. They were cycads, early pine trees that were on earth even before the Triassic period.

I gulped. It was impossible, wasn't it? My hands started to shake. It was impossible, but it had to be true!

"So where are we?" Faith demanded. Her voice was steady, but I could tell she was as freaked out as I was. She turned to Rachel. "And how did *you* get here?"

"I don't know," Rachel faltered. "I was just talking to you on Dino World, and all of sudden there was this flash of light and . . . now I'm here!"

"That's amazing! The exact same thing happened to us," Faith exclaimed. "Maybe there was some weird electrical storm, and we are dead—only we don't know it."

I wished Faith would stop talking about being dead.

"You mean we're ghosts?" Rachel breathed. Her chin began to wobble. She looked like she was about to cry. "I just want to go home!" she said in a tiny voice.

Faith turned pale. "Me, too," she whispered. Then, to my shock, tears squeezed out of the corners of her eyes. "But how will we get home if we're ghosts!" she wailed.

I looked up at the trees again. They were definitely cycads. I opened my mouth. "I don't think we're ghosts," I said slowly.

"Then what's going on?" Faith cried.

"Yeah," Rachel moaned. "Where are we?"

I swallowed. "I'm not sure," I said, hoping I was wrong. "We could be in New Mexico or maybe Montana."

"What are you talking about, Brooke?" Faith said. "I've been to New Mexico and Montana, and they don't look anything like this. New Mexico would never be this hot in October. We're definitely someplace tropical, like Florida or something."

"Why would our computers take us to Florida?" Rachel wanted to know.

"We're not in Florida," I replied grimly.

"Then where exactly are we?" Faith asked impatiently.

I took a deep breath. "I'm not sure," I said. "But I think that maybe we're . . ."

Before I could finish, something moved behind the trees in front of us. Something big. Faith's eyes popped and her mouth opened in horror.

I looked up, but even before I saw anything, I knew what it was. Something big and scaly—make that *huge* and scaly. And it was coming toward us fast!

Chapter 6

"Let's get out of here!" screamed Faith. She tugged on my arm. "Come on, Brooke! Run!" But I was paralyzed with shock. My legs would not move.

I got a good look at the gigantic creature coming toward us. It was as tall as a house and had a long snakelike neck. The greenish blue scales that covered its body gleamed in the sun as if they were wet.

I recognized it instantly: *Plateosaurus,* an early ancestor of *Apatosaurus.* I watched its huge feet hit the ground, making the tree trunks tremble. Its long neck swayed from side to side, and its big black eyes shifted this way and that, like a bird's eyes.

I was filled with terror and wonder. A real, live plateosaur was coming toward me! Any minute now it would probably crush us under its huge feet or chew us up in its giant jaws.

Then I thought of something. *Plateosaurus* didn't eat meat. It was a plant eater. If we stayed out of its path, it wouldn't hurt us. My heart in my mouth, I whispered to Faith and Rachel, "Don't move. If we run it might crush us, but if we lean against this rock, it'll just go past us."

"Are you crazy?" Faith hissed.

But Rachel nodded. "Good thinking," she murmured

stiffly. Then she flattened herself against the side of the rock. So did Faith and I.

The giant beast moved closer and closer. I started to breathe more freely. I was right. It was going to go past us. It was just looking for food.

Suddenly, out of the corner of my eye, I saw it stop. It threw back its head and sniffed. I watched in fascination. My dad had told me that paleontologists have argued for years over whether dinosaurs had a good sense of smell. Well, judging by the behavior of this one, they definitely did!

Then my blood turned to ice. The giant monster was smelling *us*! It bent its long, flexible neck. I could see its face now: big, flat, button-black eyes in a giant green, scaly face. The plateosaur opened its mouth wide. I stared transfixed at the rows of serrated teeth inside and watched, paralyzed, as the giant jaws swooped down closer and closer.

"It's going to eat us," Faith moaned.

I wondered if she was right. Perhaps the paleontologists were wrong. Maybe *Plateosaurus* hadn't eaten only plants. I closed my eyes tight. Then I felt something cold, wet, and slithery all over my face!

Chapter 7

I reared back. The plateosaur was licking me! *Oh, gross,* I thought as its giant scratchy tongue slurped across my face. I was almost too scared to breathe. I'd read somewhere that animals often licked things to see whether they were edible. *Maybe that's what this guy is doing,* I told myself wildly.

Then the enormous animal took a giant step backward. I guess I didn't taste good, because it let out a high-pitched cry and turned and thundered off through the forest. It moved so fast that the trees whipped from side to side. *Just like in a hurricane,* I thought.

"I was scared that monster was going to eat you, Brooke!" I heard Faith say beside me.

"Me, too," said Rachel, "but then I remembered . . . "

"*Plateosaurus* doesn't eat meat!" we chanted together.

"Hey," a voice behind us said. "That was amazing!"

I turned, and my mouth fell open. I couldn't believe my eyes. Billy Zipkin was coming around the other side of the rock with a big grin on his face. "Billy?" I gasped. Then I frowned. "What are you smiling about?"

"It's just all so cool!" Billy said enthusiastically. "I mean, this is the greatest dream I've ever had in my life!"

Faith, Rachel, and I looked at one another.

"Who's he?" Rachel asked in a small voice.

"His name is Billy Zipkin," I replied.

"How do you guys know each other?"

"We all go to the same school," Faith explained. "Good old Stonington Elementary—which would be a better place if Billy wasn't there," she added, only half-jokingly.

Billy stuck out his tongue at her. "That's a lie!" he said. "What Stonington needs is to get rid of dumb girls like you!"

I rolled my eyes. Even being sucked into the Internet and going back in time hadn't changed Billy Zipkin much. I wondered what he was doing here. Then a lightbulb lit up in my brain.

"So you're Zippy on line," I exclaimed. "I should have guessed!"

Billy frowned in disbelief. "You mean *you're* Dino Girl?"

"The one and only."

"Then where's Lizard Boy?" Billy asked, looking around.

My heart started thumping faster. I was asking myself the same question. If everyone else from the chat room was here, Lizard Boy had to be around somewhere. It was crazy, but as weird and terrible as our situation was, I was still looking forward to meeting him.

If anyone can get us out of this mess, Lizard Boy can! I told myself silently. "I don't know where he is," I started to answer, "but I bet—" Then Billy cut in.

"And what are you guys doing in my dream, anyway?" he demanded plaintively. "I liked it a lot better before you guys showed up. I mean, it's so neat. It's like I've actually gone back to the time of the dinosaurs."

"Uh, Billy," I said as calmly as I could, "I don't think this is a dream."

"What do you mean, it's not a dream?" Billy sputtered. "It's got to be a dream!"

I realized that, although Billy was acting as obnoxious as ever, underneath he was as freaked out as we were. He looked at me, his eyes wide.

"Give me a break. I always knew you were nuts, Brooke. But I never guessed you were such a total fruitcake," Billy almost shouted.

"Shhh," Faith pleaded nervously. "They'll hear us!"

"Who?"

"The dinosaurs," Rachel replied solemnly. Behind her glasses her eyes glinted at Billy. "And I hate to tell you this, but Brooke is right. This can't be just a dream. For one thing, if it is a dream, then we're all having the exact same one, which is impossible."

Billy turned pale. "You're kidding me, right?"

Faith and I shook our heads.

"I don't believe you."

"Look, Billy," Faith said impatiently, "if this is a dream, you had to go to sleep first, right? So what's the last thing you remember doing before you got here?"

"I—" Billy's face turned white. "I was in the Dino World chat room," he whispered hoarsely. "We were talking about *Coelophysis.*"

"Right," said Rachel. "That's what I was doing, too."

Billy licked his lips. "So where are we?" he yelped.

"I think we've gone back to the late Triassic period," I replied.

"You mean, we've somehow gone back in time millions of years?" Billy looked like he was about to burst into tears.

"I know it's crazy," I said. I felt like crying myself. "But honestly, there's no other explanation."

Billy opened his mouth and shut it; then he opened it again. "You're totally off base, Brooke," he said in a superior-sounding voice. "I don't know where we are, but no way are we in the late Triassic period."

"What makes you so sure?" I asked hotly. I knew it was dumb to feel annoyed at a time like this, but I was. Billy Zipkin was being just the same as he was at school. He couldn't admit that a bunch of girls could be right about anything.

"All the plants are right, and the dinosaurs, too," I continued. "We're on Earth about 245 million or so years ago, give or take about 20 million."

"Then why did I see a stegosaur?" Billy asked belligerently.

"Yeah, sure," I replied.

"I did! I saw a group of them over that hill. They were eating a bunch of big pink flowers."

"Pink flowers?"

"Yup." Billy gave me a triumphant look. "Magnolias, which, for your information, didn't appear on Earth until the late Jurassic period, long after the Triassic had ended. I used my laptop to identify them."

"Your *laptop*?" Faith, Rachel, and I all shouted at the same time.

"You mean, you have your computer here?" I asked Billy.

"Not my computer, my laptop," Billy corrected me. "It was in my backpack, which was hooked around my foot when my computer exploded," he explained sheepishly.

"But I don't get it. How can your laptop work here?" Faith wanted to know.

"Battery pack," the rest of us answered automatically.

Faith was obviously the only one among us who wasn't a computer nut.

I looked back at Billy. "So how did your laptop help you figure out the pink flowers were magnolias?" I asked sharply.

Billy shrugged. "I just logged on to the Dino World library."

"The Dino World library," I screeched. "Get out the laptop, Billy. If you can get into Dino World, maybe we can make contact with someone, tell them we're stuck here."

Billy shook his head. "Won't work. I tried it," he said in a flat voice. "I kept asking if anyone was there, but no one was. In the chat room, I mean. I wasn't that surprised, because I thought this whole thing was a dream, and stuff like that always happens in dreams." He gestured at the backpack beside him. "But you can give it a try if you want."

I didn't wait for a second invitation. I unzipped Billy's backpack and hauled out his laptop. It was a beautiful machine. Brand-new. I quickly flicked it on and tried to log on to the Net.

But I couldn't log on the way I usually did. No matter what icon I hit, the same thing always came up on the screen: the home page of Dino World. I accessed the chat room and typed in *Hello, hello, anyone there?* But just as Billy had said, there was no answer.

I double clicked on the Dino World library icon. I pulled *magnolia* onto the screen and then *Stegosaurus.* Billy was right on his timing in both cases. Both the flower and the dinosaur lived in the late Jurassic period. There was no way *Stegosaurus* and magnolias could have coexisted with *Coelophysis* and *Plateosaurus,* which thrived millions of years earlier in the late Triassic period.

I looked up to see Billy grinning at me victoriously.

"See, Brooke," he said. "I told you so. No way are we in the late Triassic period."

"But we can't be in the Jurassic period. We saw a plateosaurus running around," Rachel said softly.

Billy smirked at her. "Good point. So we must be in a dream."

I shook my head. "This is not a dream!"

"Then it's something else," Billy countered. "Maybe we're in outer space. Maybe we're on some alien planet, and the aliens are making us think that we're on Earth millions of years ago."

"Or maybe the scientists have it wrong," Faith said gloomily. "Maybe Earth was all mixed up like this, and we just don't know it."

I frowned. Both Billy and Faith might be right. Then I shook my head. "I don't think we're in outer space," I said with assurance.

Faith shot me a look. "Why are you so sure?" she asked.

I shrugged my shoulders. I didn't know why, but somehow I knew this place was for real. I shivered. "It's just logical," I said stubbornly. "I mean, what are the chances of another planet being so much like Earth? Why would a bunch of aliens be interested in us? Whatever is happening to us has to have something to do with dinosaurs."

"I think you're right, Dino Girl," Rachel piped up. "But I still don't understand it."

"And if we're not in outer space, how can you be sure the past wasn't like this?" Faith added. "Why couldn't *Stegosaurus* and *Plateosaurus* have lived at the same time?"

"Because scientists have been studying the fossil

record for years," Billy explained. "The fossils of those two dinosaurs never, ever appear in the same time line." Then his face went pale again. "But if we're not in outer space and we're not in the Triassic or the Jurassic, where are we?" he asked in a high, scared-sounding voice. "And how are we going to get home?"

No one knew the answer.

I gazed up at the endlessly blue sky. A large shadow fell across it. I squinted up and saw a giant winged shape hovering above the trees. A bird! Then my heart sank. It wasn't a bird like any I'd ever seen.

It was *Pteranodon,* a kind of pterodactyl. More and more shadows joined the first one. I squinted harder. A whole flock of pteranodons was flying above our heads.

My photographic memory called up what my favorite dinosaur book said about pterodactyls: "Vultures of the Mesozoic era, they hunted fish and feasted on carcasses left by carnivorous dinosaurs. They might have circled above their prey as today's vultures do."

I squinted at the gigantic, birdlike creatures again. They were circling above us, swooping down closer and closer as if they knew we were goners!

"Come on," I said sharply. "We've got to get out of here. Billy, you'd better put your laptop away. We might need to use it later. But right now, we've got to find some shelter. It isn't safe here."

"You can say that again," Billy squeaked. He picked up his laptop and stuffed it into his backpack. Then he shouldered the pack in a hurry. "Let's get going!" he added, eyeing the pterodactyls nervously. "There's a low mountain over that way, with lots of rocky canyons around it. I thought I saw the entrance to a cave there. Maybe we could hide inside it."

"Good idea," I agreed. "You lead the way."

"Okay." Billy glanced up at the pterodactyls again, and then he scowled. "We're definitely not in the Jurassic period, either," he commented. "*Pteranodon* didn't appear until the late Cretaceous. I don't get it. Everything's all mixed up!"

If only Lizard Boy were here, I murmured to myself. *Maybe he could help us figure out what's going on.*

Then I stopped in my tracks. *Where is Lizard Boy? Why isn't he here when everyone else from Dino World is?* I couldn't figure out any reason, unless—my heart skipped a beat—something had happened to him.

"Brooke, what are you waiting for?" Faith nudged me. "Those bird things are getting closer. We've got to get going. Now!"

I looked up. The pterodactyls were hovering in the sky just above us now. I sucked in my breath. They were bigger than I had ever imagined. Each one was the length of a small truck. Their beaks looked as sharp as knives.

I covered my head as one dive-bombed down on us. It came so close, I could feel the air from its wings beating over me like a huge wave.

Faith was right. We had to move fast.

Chapter 8

"Which way, Billy?" Faith screamed.

"This way. Follow me!"

Billy took Faith by the arm and pushed her through the trees. Rachel and I followed. We felt safer there, under the branches. But I could hear insects, slithery noises, and, far away, a sound like thunder—but it wasn't thunder.

It was dinosaurs walking. Some were running!

I ran into a faceful of leaves. Ouch! They felt sharp and thorny. "Are you sure you're going the right way, Billy?" I demanded. "I feel like we're going in circles."

"No, I just spotted a bunch of rocks sticking up over there. This is right."

I yelped as a pteranodon swooped down at us again.

"Owww!" Faith cried ahead of me.

I stared. Her hand was bleeding. The tip of a pteranodon beak had pierced her skin. My heart started thudding faster. Although the cut didn't look too deep, this was very bad news. My dad had told me that if dinosaurs did have a sense of smell, they probably used it the way other animals did—to look for prey. He said the smell of blood always attracted predators. It was a rule of nature.

"Faith, wrap up your hand in this," I commanded, pulling a bandanna out of my pocket. I helped her tie the square of cotton tightly over the cut. Meanwhile, the pterodactyls circled down—lower and lower.

"Come on, Billy, show us where to go—and hurry!" I screamed.

Billy blindly blundered ahead. The rest of us followed, running along as fast as we could. But all we saw were trees and more trees, crisscrossed by quick-running streams and creeks.

Normally, I would have stopped to admire the beautiful landscape. But I wasn't thinking about natural beauty right then. I was thinking that if we didn't find Billy's cave soon, we would all be pterodactyl dinners!

"Over there!" Billy panted.

I pushed away some giant leaves. *Gingko leaves,* I thought. Then I wrinkled up my forehead. *How in the world did I know that?* I wondered. I was pretty sure I'd never seen pictures of the giant leaves before. So why did they feel so . . . familiar?

"Brooke, look!" Faith nudged me.

I looked and gasped. A volcanic mountain rose above us. "It isn't very high yet, because the world is so young," I murmured under my breath. Then I shivered. It was odd how here, in this place, I kept seeing things that felt familiar. *It's just because I've studied dinosaurs so much,* I told myself.

I gazed up at the volcano. I could see the mouth of a cave poking out between some jagged rocks about halfway up.

With a burst of new energy, we sped ahead. The pterodactyls weren't swooping so close now. They were moving away, after something else. I wondered what it could be. Then I heard a terrible roaring behind and below us. I turned and saw two huge monsters fighting. One was an apatosaur. The other was a tyrannosaur!

I shuddered. The *T. rex* was a quarter of a mile away, but it was so big, it looked as if it were right on top of us. It leaped up at the even bigger dove gray apatosaur.

Faith moaned. "The poor thing," she cried.

It was true. The apatosaur did look gentle, almost beautiful, beside the leering face of *T. rex*. As we watched in horror, the fierce meat eater dragged the apatosaur down. Then, with weird, bloodcurdling cries, the pterodactyls swooped down to get their share of the feast.

I shuddered again. The death of the apatosaur meant the pterodactyls would leave us alone for a while. But we had to get to shelter soon. Before long, all the monsters around us would be hungry again.

I gazed at the clear sky. The sun was sinking.

Night was the dinosaurs' favorite hunting time. Lizard Boy was always saying that. He insisted it was true, even when other kids on Dino World pointed out that scientists had no way of knowing that for sure.

All dinosaurs hunted better at night. I could remember Lizard Boy typing out those very words. I only hoped he was wrong. If he wasn't, we were in big trouble.

If only we could find Lizard Boy, I thought. I felt sure he could help us understand what was happening. Then a strange and terrifying thought crossed my mind— *unless Lizard Boy is behind all this.*

"Brooke, don't slow down now!" Faith tugged on my arm. "Look, there's Billy's cave, right up there." My adrenaline rising, I followed the others over the jagged lava rocks. My feet ached, but I didn't care. We would soon be safe in the cave. I scrambled quickly up the steep mountainside after Faith and Rachel and Billy. We reached the mouth of the cave together.

"Come on, let's hurry up and go in," I urged, glancing over my shoulder. "The pterodactyls are coming back again."

I took a step forward, but Billy yanked me back. I stopped and peered into the dark mouth of the cave. Then I saw why.

Gleaming at us from the depths of the cavern was a pair of glowing red eyes!

Chapter 9

I heard a hissing sound. Billy and Rachel leaped to one side of the cave opening. Faith and I leaped to the other. The red eyes followed us. As the creature moved into the light, my heart almost stopped beating.

It was a snake at least sixty feet long. An ancient python!

"Faith, run!" I shouted.

She raced backward. I did, too. We ran as fast as we could, but we weren't fast enough. In seconds, the giant python had encircled us. I could feel its thick, horny scales pressing against me from all sides. It was getting harder and harder to breathe. My best friend and I were being squeezed to death. "Help!" I gasped.

I saw a flash in front of me. Then I blinked. Billy was flashing a bright light—a flashlight—in the python's eyes.

The python hissed and loosened its grip; then it coiled around us even tighter. The sky overhead seemed to go dark.

"Brooke, I can't breathe," Faith panted.

"I can't either!" I puffed.

I was sure that in moments we would be dead. Suddenly I heard the sound of wings beating. The horrible scales around me loosened. The python hissed and reared up. I couldn't understand why.

Then I saw what was happening.

It was the pterodactyls! They'd come to get *us,* but, instead, they had stumbled on the giant python. They swarmed the python's head, stabbing at it over and over with their sharp, curved beaks. The python whizzed around, lashing out at the pterodactyls again and again. Then it became very still.

Faith and I cautiously eased out from under its huge body and fled into the darkness of the cave. Billy and Rachel were already there. We hid behind a large boulder and watched as the flock of pterodactyls lifted the body of the snake high into the air. After a moment, they dropped it down onto the plain below. Then they began to feast.

"Whew," Faith gasped. "I thought I was going to be squeezed to death for sure."

"I can't believe you guys are alive," Rachel said.

"Me, either," Billy agreed.

"I can't believe you thought of flashing your light in the python's eyes," I exclaimed, turning to Billy. "The python was pretty surprised, too. He forgot to squeeze for a minute."

"Yeah," Faith piped up. "You might have saved our lives, Billy!"

"Where'd you get the flashlight, anyway?" I asked.

Billy shrugged, but I could tell he was proud of himself. "I always carry one in my backpack," he said coolly. "It's like my Boy Scout leader says, 'It pays to be prepared.'"

"Well, it sure startled that snake," Rachel remarked.

"And the pterodactyls," I added.

"Maybe if we shine Billy's flashlight tonight, we can keep the dinosaurs away," Faith suggested.

"Or maybe it'll just let them know where we are," Billy muttered gloomily. He peered out at the horizon. The sun looked like a giant orange. It was sinking fast. Billy frowned. I knew what he was thinking.

When night came, the dinosaurs would come out to hunt in force. There would be nowhere to hide.

I glanced around the cave. It was large, but not as large as I had expected. I breathed deeply. *Phew!* It smelled like rotten eggs. I looked around for the source of the disgusting smell and found it minutes later. Huge broken eggshells lay near the back of the cave.

Faith made a face. "What are all these yucky broken eggs doing here? They must have come from some pretty big chickens."

Rachel smiled. "They're not chicken eggs, Faith," she said kindly. "They're dinosaur eggs."

Faith turned green. "Oh, gross! What are they doing here?"

"The python probably stole them from dinosaur nests," I said. "A lot of ancient snakes lived on dinosaur eggs."

Faith held her nose. "Well, I think they're disgusting."

"I think they're cool." Billy picked up an egg that wasn't broken. It was the size of a small cantaloupe.

"What are you doing?" I asked as he carefully placed the egg in his backpack.

"I'm collecting specimens," Billy replied solemnly. "If we ever get out of here, I want to have something to prove I was really here. If I can take back a real dinosaur egg, I'll be world famous!"

"If we ever get out of here," Faith reminded him.

Billy just scooped up another unbroken egg and then another. He carefully nestled them in his backpack.

"I can't believe you still have room in that thing," Rachel remarked, staring at Billy's bulging pack. "Do you carry that huge pack around every day?"

"Yup. It's extra, extra large," Billy replied smugly. "It's like my Boy Scout leader always says—"

"I don't think I want to hear more words of wisdom from your Boy Scout leader," Faith grumped. "I'm hungry!"

"Yeah, so am I," I said. I glanced over at Billy. "I wish you had something to eat in that backpack."

"Or drink," Faith piped up. "I'm so thirsty!"

"Me too," Rachel agreed. "I guess that proves this can't be a dream," she added glumly. "I never get hungry or thirsty when I'm dreaming."

"I think I do have something to drink in here," Billy mumbled. He rummaged around and pulled out a bottle of Gatorade. I made a face. Gatorade isn't my favorite drink, but I was so thirsty I think warm pond water would have tasted great. We each took a sip from the bottle. Then Billy pulled out a package of licorice. We ate one stick each. Not exactly a square meal, but it was better than nothing.

"Is that all you've got?" Faith asked.

"I have my lunch from school," Billy replied awkwardly.

"Let's share it," I said eagerly.

Billy reluctantly pulled a crumbled-up paper bag from the bottom of his backpack. It smelled like . . . fish!

"Leftover fish sticks?" Faith cried. "You eat leftover fish sticks for lunch?"

Billy blushed. "My mom packs my lunches," he

explained. "She has weird ideas about what kids like."

I almost felt sorry for him. With a mom who packed lunches like that, no wonder Billy Zipkin was such a nerd. I took a small bite of a fish stick. It didn't taste too good. "They're not so bad," I said politely.

"At least not when you're starving and stuck in a dinosaur time warp," Faith added, gulping one down.

"I've never eaten a fish stick before," Rachel mused between bites. "I guess you could get to like them in two hundred million years or so."

We all cracked up. Then we peeked out of the mouth of the cave and became serious again. Darkness was settling over the valley. I knew that when that happened, we would be in a zillion times more danger.

"There's nothing we can do now but wait 'til morning," Billy reasoned. He put the bottle of Gatorade back in his backpack. As he did, I spotted his laptop.

"Hey, Billy," I said. "Can I fool around with your computer for a few minutes?"

Billy hesitated. "Sure, I guess. But don't spend too much time on it. The battery is getting low."

"I won't."

I pulled the laptop out of the backpack and flicked it on. Just as before, the Dino World home page came up. Now I couldn't access the chat room at all. I clicked the mouse to go to the library instead. I had visited the Dino World library a few times before, but I'd never really appreciated how much information there was in it.

"Wow, this is unbelievable!" I cried, scrolling through the electronic card catalogue. "I've never seen this many books on dinosaurs listed anywhere. And check this out. They even have a computer re-creation of how dinosaurs became extinct."

"How did it happen?" Faith asked.

"This asteroid hit Earth and—*boom*!" Billy answered for me.

"And they all died, just like that?" Faith demanded.

"No, dummy," Billy said sharply. Then his face softened. "Well, actually, a lot of them probably did. But the asteroid changed the climate of Earth, and they starved or something. It's pretty complicated."

"I could run the re-creation for you if you want," I offered.

Faith shuddered. "No, thanks. Just thinking about dinosaurs is too creepy right now," she said softly. "And thinking about giant asteroids is even creepier."

I thought of the ball of flame bursting out of my computer, the ball of flame that had sucked us into this place. "Yeah," I agreed. I clicked on the heading *Dinosaur Information* instead. The screen wavered. Billy was right; the battery was getting low.

"Maybe you'd better switch it off," Faith said anxiously.

"Yeah, turn it off!" Billy sounded nervous.

"I will in a minute," I promised. "I just want to look at something." I clicked on *Coelophysis*. Instantly a picture of the small, meat-eating dinosaur appeared on-screen. I read the text beneath the picture: Coelophysis, *the earliest known ancestor of the later, better known meateaters, from the giant* Tyrannosaurus *to the small, agile* Troödon. Troödon *is believed to be the most direct descendant of* Coelophysis.

"*Troödon,*" I murmured aloud. It was a dinosaur name I knew I'd heard before, but for some reason I couldn't remember what *Troödon* looked like.

Faith lifted her head. "What about her?" she asked.

"Who?"

"Mrs. Trowdon. Didn't you just say her name?"

"No," I replied. Then I frowned.

Troödon. Trowdon. The words sounded almost exactly the same. It could be a coincidence. But somehow I didn't think so. I looked down at the computer screen again.

Troödon *is believed to be the most direct descendant of* Coelophysis, the text read.

I gulped. So *Troödon* and *Coelophysis* were close relatives. I thought of the model we'd seen in the secondhand store, the feathered model of *Coelophysis.* We'd been talking about that model of *Coelophysis* when we had been sucked into the computer, sucked back in time. I wrinkled my forehead, trying to remember exactly what had been going on.

Billy had been asking Faith the name of the store where we had found the model. And Lizard Boy hadn't wanted Faith to tell him. Lizard Boy had interrupted Faith twice, trying to stop her from giving the name of the store.

What did Lizard Boy have to do with Fossils? Or with Mrs. Trowdon? What, if anything, did Mrs. Trowdon have to do with *Troödon* the dinosaur? Somewhere, somehow, there had to be a connection.

I leaned over Billy's laptop and continued reading.

Chapter 10

"*Troödon* lived in the late Cretaceous period," I read aloud. "*Troödon* was very fast-moving and had a much larger brain than any other dinosaur. Scientists believe *Troödon* hunted at night, was a social creature, and lived in large herds. *Troödon* cared for its young. Scientists are especially interested in *Troödon* because they believe the dinosaur offers clues about how dinosaurs might have evolved if they hadn't become extinct. Some scientists think that, in time *Troödon* might have grown into intelligent lizard creatures—lizard people."

The words on the screen began to jump up and down. I caught my breath.

"Stop reading, Brooke," Faith snapped. "You're going to use up the battery. I don't see why you need to learn more about dinosaurs from some dumb computer anyway. Not when they're all around us." She shivered. "Come on. Billy says we should pile up rocks around the entrance of the cave so the dinosaurs will be less likely to find us."

I switched off the laptop, put it back in Billy's pack, and scrambled to my feet. Rachel, Faith, and Billy were already working to block the cave entrance with piles of medium-sized boulders.

"Don't block it all the way," I instructed. "Just enough to hide the mouth of the cave. Leave us room to get out. We might have to make a quick escape or something."

Faith's eyes met mine. "Good point," she agreed. Then her eyes misted over and she blinked. "Oh, Brooke, this is so awful," she whispered. She gulped hard. "I hope we get back home."

"Me, too," I said softly.

Faith tried to smile. "I bet. You wouldn't want to miss the dance, would you?"

I grinned. I knew Faith was joking. Every time there was a school dance, Faith wanted me to go, but I never did. "Oh, yeah," I replied. "I'd really hate to miss it."

Faith shook her head. "It's weird," she murmured. "I keep thinking about that model."

"What about it?"

"It's what got us here." Faith lowered her voice. "Mrs. Trowdon and that store have something to do with this. I can feel it in my bones. I just can't figure out what."

"Neither can I," I whispered. So Faith had reached the same conclusions I had. No wonder we were best friends.

"If only your friend Lizard Boy would show up," Faith continued. "Maybe he could help us figure out what's going on."

"Yeah," I said weakly. I'd been hoping Lizard Boy would show up ever since we'd landed here. I'd been thinking all along that if anyone could rescue us, he could. But now I wasn't so sure.

I didn't want to believe Lizard Boy was behind this incredible journey of ours. But I couldn't help thinking that we should have met up with him by now. Why had he tried so hard to stop Faith from mentioning Fossils by name? I frowned. I had a lot of questions, but no answers.

Lizard Boy has to be behind this, I thought. What other explanation was there?

That still left two big questions: *why* and *how*?

I took a deep breath and glanced around the cave. "Lizard Boy, where are you?" I murmured desperately under my breath. "I thought we were friends."

I peered out of the mouth of the cave. The sky was a clear midnight blue. Suddenly I caught my breath. There were so many stars! I'd never seen a sky like this, not even when I had camped out. There were a zillion more stars in the sky than I'd ever imagined. It was so beautiful, my mouth fell open.

I felt strange and sad. So this was what the world had been like before there were people. No bright lights, no air pollution, no smog. Just a zillion stars and a huge, silver moon.

Then I shuddered. It was beautiful except for one thing. Shadows had fallen across the plain below us. Huge, ominous shadows. Dinosaurs out hunting!

Chapter 11

"What are they?" Faith hissed.

I didn't answer. I just sucked in my breath as two huge shadows came into view.

"Uh-oh," Billy squeaked.

"Tyrannosaurus!" Rachel breathed.

I had seen models of *Tyrannosaurus* in museums. But they hadn't prepared me for this. These dinosaurs were total monsters. We were staring at the hugest, most fearsome predators ever to roam Earth!

They moved forward quickly on their powerful hind legs, walking upright, almost the way people walk. Only they were much taller than people. Each one was as tall as a two-story house. As they prowled along, the moonlight glinted on their scaly heads and sparkled off their long, shiny teeth.

I shuddered, remembering that the head of this meat eater was four feet long, only a little shorter than I was. And each *Tyrannosaurus* tooth was seven inches long!

The bigger of the two dinosaurs turned to the other and made a low growling sound. A rush of fear shot through my body. The noise the big *T. rex* made was somewhere between a bird call and the cry of an angry, starving animal. It sounded like a call to war!

"Keep very still," Billy warned softly. "No one move, or they'll spot us."

We pressed ourselves against the walls of the cave. A cloud passed over the moon. The sky darkened. Then the wind blew the cloud away, and the moonlight seemed to glow over the landscape even more brightly than before.

The bigger *T. rex* let out another bloodcurdling cry. Both dinosaurs lifted their heads and swiveled their huge, glowing eyes toward the mouth of the cave. They were staring straight at us. They opened their mouths, showing their razor-sharp teeth.

"Uh-oh!" Faith murmured.

The bigger *T. rex* leaned forward and sniffed the air. Its eyes widened; then its tongue flickered out between rows of shining teeth. It made another growling noise. Only this time, it sounded happy. The smaller *T. rex* roared contentedly. They both started up the mountain.

A few minutes later, I heard rocks falling, dislodged by their giant claws. The two dinosaurs were moving fast, coming closer, closer. I shut my eyes, afraid to look. Then I heard a loud scratching.

I opened my eyes slowly and gasped.

The big *T. rex* was at the mouth of the cave. Its eyes gazed into mine. Its teeth were bared, and its clawed forelimbs stretched toward me and my friends. It flung its head back and let out a long, triumphant howl.

The four of us jumped backward.

The *T. rex* pushed against the boulders we'd piled up around the mouth of the cave. It tossed one aside as easily as if it were a foam pillow.

My heart started thumping. The dinosaur and its mate were going to eat us. There was no way we could stop them.

"Run!" Billy shrieked.

Chapter 12

We ran, but there was nowhere to go except to the back of the cave. We crouched in the darkness against the wall. The big tyrannosaur was still scrabbling at the boulders at the mouth of the cave. We could hear rocks crashing together, tumbling down the mountainside.

Rays of moonlight pierced the inky darkness in the cave. Faith squeezed my hand. "Brooke, I'm scared!" she whispered.

I wasn't just scared; I was terrified. Any minute, the monster would be inside the cave. The worst predator that ever lived was going to have us for dinner. We didn't stand a chance.

Think, I told myself frantically. *Do something.* But my brain was frozen. What could four kids do against two hungry, seventy-ton dinosaurs?

I closed my eyes tight. Then I heard a strange sound, a low, musical, hooting noise. It sounded familiar somehow, like the sound the barn owls make on summer nights. For some weird reason, the sound was even more familiar than that to me. I kept thinking I had heard it somewhere before—maybe in a dream or something. I opened my eyes and pricked up my ears.

The hooting was getting louder. The dinosaurs heard

it too. The big *T. rex* stopped tearing at the mouth of the cave. It lifted its head. Then its horrible jaws curved up, as if it were smiling.

I held my breath as the huge monster turned and thundered away down the side of the volcano. After a moment, the smaller *T. rex* stalked after its mate.

"What's going on?" Faith cried.

"Yeah, where are they going?" Billy asked shakily.

"I have no idea," I replied.

Rachel's eyes gleamed behind her glasses. "Let's go look," she said. I stared at her in shock. I couldn't believe she wanted to go look out the mouth of the cave with two monster dinosaurs out there.

"What are you, nuts?" Billy hissed.

But Rachel just turned and tiptoed toward the cave mouth. I gazed after her admiringly. For someone who looked like a junior librarian, Rachel was pretty brave.

"Rachel, stop!" I whispered. But she just kept going. I sighed and tiptoed after her. I knew it was crazy to go to the mouth of the cave. But, like Rachel, I was curious. I wanted to see what was going on. What in the world had made the two dinosaurs take off like that? And what was making that hooting noise? I pricked up my ears again. The hooting was louder and louder, yet it was still somehow soothing and pleasant.

I crept up beside Rachel and peered out over the moonlit landscape. Two small, slender dinosaurs were moving slowly across the valley below us, making hooting noises as they went.

"Twwwoooo, twooo," they gurgled, stopping from time to time to glance behind them. One of them was limping as if it was hurt. And stalking after them were the two giant tyrannosaurs!

The tyrannosaurs' claws were curved in front of them. Their expressions were greedy, bloodthirsty. They were moving rapidly across the valley, closing in on the slender dinosaurs. But the two small dinosaurs didn't seem to know they were in great danger.

Hurry, I told the two little dinosaurs silently. *Don't you see those monsters coming after you? Hurry!*

The little dinosaur with the limp stopped in its tracks. It stood up on its hind legs. *"Twooo!"* it gurgled sadly. Then I saw its eyes shining in the moonlight. Its eyes didn't look scared. They looked intelligent, calculating.

Suddenly I recognized what kind of dinosaur it was— a troödont. I remembered that *Troödon* was believed to have been the smartest dinosaur that ever lived. But the way these two small troödonts were acting didn't seem very smart.

"Twooo!" they hooted again.

The bigger *T. rex* let out a fearsome roar. With dazzling speed, the tyrannosaurs sprinted forward, moving across the valley to surround the small, helpless dinosaurs on both sides.

Fear clenched my heart. The tyrannosaurs were almost upon them. The two troödonts were going to be ripped apart!

Suddenly I heard hooting all around us, hooting from behind all the trees and shrubs in the valley, hooting from all over the mountainside. Then I heard a loud, thundering sound. Boulders came raining down on the valley from all sides. The hooting got louder.

"Twooo, twoo!" It sounded like laughter.

I blinked. The bigger *T. rex* was lying on its side. The back of its head had been crushed by a giant boulder. Its huge eyes stared blindly at the moon.

My heart started racing. The big *T. rex* was dead!

The other tyrannosaur let out a bone-chilling yowl. It started to run, but dark shapes streaked down the mountain slope on all sides.

The shapes were hundreds of troödonts. They moved swiftly, efficiently, as if each of them knew exactly where to go. They circled around the smaller *T. rex,* blocking its escape. I realized they were driving the ferocious dinosaur into a narrow rocky pass between two high stone walls. The *T. rex* screamed as the troödonts circled closer and closer, slicing at its with their small, sharp claws and pointed teeth. The dinosaur ran into the narrow rocky pass.

More boulders came crashing down. Minutes later we heard the terrible, high-pitched cry of a dying animal. The second *T. rex* was dead.

The hills echoed with the low, musical hooting I had heard earlier. Then everything became silent. Very silent.

As we watched from the mouth of the cave, the troödonts stripped the dead dinosaurs clean of meat. They worked quickly and calmly, each one doing just what it needed to do. Watching them gave me the creeps. It was as if they'd planned the attack ahead of time. Or maybe they knew how to communicate without sound.

The pack finished their work. Then, at exactly the same moment, they all swiveled their heads toward the mouth of the cave. Faith, Billy, Rachel, and I sat crouched in terror.

Their yellow eyes peered up at us. A hundred troödonts blinked at exactly the same moment. Then they started toward us.

Chapter 13

No one said anything about running this time. We knew it would do no good—we were hopelessly outnumbered. We stared into the troödonts' yellow eyes as if we'd been hypnotized. They came scrambling up the side of the volcano toward us. Their golden eyes winked at us like hundreds of tiny flashlights. I noticed their scaly skin—yellow scales with gray bands around them.

I shivered. Then I thought of Mrs. Trowdon and her son again. *Troödon, Trowdon.* It couldn't be just a coincidence.

Somehow these small, intelligent dinosaurs were connected to Mrs. Trowdon, her son, and the model of *Coelophysis* that Faith and I had stumbled upon in Fossils. And somehow they were all connected to Lizard Boy and the mystery of why we were here.

But how?

I wrinkled up my forehead, thinking hard. But there was no time to think. The troödonts were already at the mouth of the cave. With rising terror, I saw their long, thin, scaly limbs reaching toward us. Their claws looked like hands with three fingers.

I tried to back away, but it was too late. One of the troödonts sprinted forward and grabbed me!

I felt myself being lifted into the air.

I wanted to scream, but I knew that wouldn't help anything. The troödonts surrounded us totally. Three of them were holding me. Two big, brightly striped ones had hoisted Faith up into the air. Another two were holding on to Billy. Rachel hadn't been caught yet, but three troödonts were circling around her.

There was no escape.

My teeth started to chatter as the troödonts carried me out of the cave, then roughly carted me down the mountainside. The dinosaurs were taking us somewhere. But where? I rolled my eyes around.

I could hear Faith screaming. "Put me down!" she yelled, kicking her legs as hard as she could. "Put me down this minute, you creepy old lizards!"

I almost smiled. *Trust Faith to put up a good fight, even when things are hopeless,* I thought dimly. I wondered where the troödonts were taking us. *If they were going to kill us, why didn't they just do it and get it over with?*

We moved along faster and faster, so fast that the world rushed past in a big blur. I felt as if I were about to faint. Suddenly everything stopped moving and my feet touched solid ground again.

I glanced around. I was standing next to Faith, Billy, and Rachel. We were in a rocky cave halfway down the mountainside. The floor of the cave was smooth and sandy. The walls sloped up gently, almost like the grandstand in a sports arena. I had a feeling the troödonts often gathered here, because hundreds of them were lined up along the sloping walls above us at that moment.

My heart in my mouth, I looked at the silent, expressionless lizard faces, their pointy jaws, their sharp teeth, their gleaming yellow eyes. Their eyes reminded me of something. Then I realized what it was—Mrs. Trowdon and her son. Their eyes were exactly the same as the eyes of these lizards.

Trowdon, Troödon. How were they related? Mrs. Trowdon was weird, but she was definitely a person. These creatures were dinosaurs, prehistoric reptiles.

I shivered and lifted my head. A troödont was standing right in front of me. It was bigger than the others. It looked older, too. Its gray stripes had faded to a soft, yellowish brown, and even its eyes did not gleam as brightly as the other dinosaurs' did. Nevertheless, the troödont's gaze was intense. I flinched as its big, yellow eyes gripped mine.

Why was this old lizard just staring at me like this?

Then the eyes blinked, and I heard something. It was like words, only it wasn't words. It was like a thought planted in my brain.

Welcome, Daughter, said a male voice. But the voice didn't say it, not aloud anyway. I gazed sharply at the big lizard. His eyes were still fixed on my face.

"What are you talking about?" I murmured.

Don't you know? You are one of us, he answered.

Chapter 14

I stared at the big lizard in shock. His wide mouth was turned up at the corners as if he were smiling at me.

I swallowed hard. Was I losing my mind? No way could this lizard be talking to me. I had to be imagining it. Then I heard another younger-sounding voice in my head.

Old One, what should we do with them? it asked impatiently.

Other voices picked up the question. *Yes, Old One, what should we do with them? Tell us, tell us what to do!*

I watched the big troödont, Old One. He had turned his head away from me and was gazing up at the other dinosaurs. I shivered. They all looked as if they were thinking hard, talking over some important question, only their mouths weren't moving.

Old One, we need to decide! What should we do with them?

This time the words rang through my head so clearly, I was sure I couldn't be imagining them. *Was I going crazy, or was I reading the dinosaurs' minds?*

Kill them. That's what Lizard Boy said to do, said the young, impatient-sounding voice.

Why should we kill them when we've eaten already? a female voice replied.

Lizard Boy said they deserve to be killed. He said in the time of our children's children's children, they will kill us!

I stared at the troödonts in amazement. Their mouths weren't moving. Their faces were perfectly still. So why was I imagining they were saying words? I was totally losing it. That was the only possible explanation. I was so scared, I was going nuts.

I looked at Faith. Her face was pale, and her mouth was set in a thin line. She looked frightened and confused. Her eyes met mine. "What's going on?" she mouthed at me. "Why aren't they doing anything?"

I shook my head, "I don't know," I mouthed back, my heart sinking. Faith obviously wasn't hearing any voices, and neither was Rachel or Billy. Only I was. *So kill them,* a chorus of voices cried in my mind.

The big old dinosaur's yellow eyes fixed on mine again. He gazed at me for a long time. His eyes bored deep into mine. I couldn't understand it. I should have been terrified, but I wasn't. I felt as if I knew the old lizard. I felt as if I knew his eyes.

Eyes like Mrs. Trowdon's. Eyes like her son's. I gasped. Eyes like mine, and my mother's. Amber eyes.

No! the big troödont said. It was like he was talking inside my head. *No, we must not hurt them.*

Why not? asked a smaller one.

The old dinosaur didn't answer right away. He slowly stretched out his three-fingered claw and touched me on the forehead. *Because she has the memory!*

I heard him say that, clear as a bell. I knew he'd said it, even though his mouth hadn't moved, even though he hadn't made a single sound. I was sure that was what he said. I just couldn't understand what he meant. I "had the memory"?

Were these dinosaurs going to spare our lives because I had a photographic memory? It didn't make any sense!

I opened my eyes wider. The big troödont was still touching me on the forehead with his claw, only now his head was bowed. The other troödonts had their heads bowed, too. I heard words echoing around me. *Leave them alone! She has the memory! She has the memory!*

All at once, the troödonts backed away. I hardly dared breathe as they turned and slipped silently into the night. In moments, they were swallowed up by the darkness.

I couldn't believe it. They were gone, and we were alone in the sheltered rocky cave. I opened my mouth. "Are you guys all right?" I whispered, turning to Faith, Billy, and Rachel.

"Yeah, I think so," Billy replied. He shuddered. "I thought they were going to kill us!"

"Me, too," Rachel said miserably. "I can't understand why they didn't. It was like something stopped them at the last minute. Something made them change their minds."

I swallowed, pondering what I'd heard. *Leave them alone. She has the memory.* What could it mean?

Then I saw Faith staring at me. "What is it?" I said. Something about the way she was looking at me made my blood run cold.

"Brooke!" she yelped. "What's happening to you?"

"What are you talking about?" I looked down at myself, and my jaw dropped. My arms and my legs were covered with scales! Yellowy scales with gray stripes running through them. Even my hands had changed.

Instead of five fingers I now had three, each one ending in a sharp claw.

"Brooke, you've turned into one of them!" Faith shrieked, and she burst into loud sobs.

Chapter 15

I stared at my hands in horror. They weren't my hands. They were claws—*Troödon* claws! "Oh, no," I gasped. I reached up and touched my face. With claws instead of fingers, I couldn't be sure, but it felt like my regular old face.

"Is—is my face the same?" I stammered.

"Yeah," Faith croaked, "but your arms, your legs . . . "

I breathed a sigh of relief. At least I hadn't turned into a total monster. *At least, not yet,* I told myself.

I thought about the way the troödonts had surrounded us, the way they had watched me with their gleaming yellow eyes, what I had heard them thinking: *Leave them alone. She has the memory.*

I began to tremble. I felt really scared. Then I saw Billy Zipkin staring at me. He looked scared, but he also looked disgusted. "I knew you were behind this, Brooke," he said softly.

"Behind what?" I gasped. "What are you talking about?"

Billy's eyes rested on my hands. "Behind us being here," he replied sullenly. "Behind us being trapped here with all these monsters. You're one of them, Brooke, aren't you?" He stormed out of the cave.

For some crazy reason, I felt guilty. Had Billy guessed that I had somehow known what the troödonts were thinking? "Billy, don't be ridiculous," I said pleadingly as I followed him outside. Faith and Rachel ran after me. "I'm not one of them. I swear. I don't know any more about why we're here than you do."

"Then why did the troödonts leave us alone when they saw you?" Billy demanded. "And why are you turning into one of them?"

"Billy, stop it!" Faith cut in coldly. "Can't you see Brooke is as frightened and confused as the rest of us? It's not her fault this happened."

"Yeah," Rachel said solemnly. "We have to be scientific about this."

Billy's mouth turned down at the corners. "What's scientific about her turning into a gross lizard?" he snapped.

A wave of anger passed over me. I glared at Billy. Then, in a flash, I realized why he was being so nasty. Billy was terrified.

I glanced over at Faith and then at Rachel. They were both sticking up for me, but I could see that they were scared and puzzled, too. They must have noticed the same thing Billy had: that the troödonts had backed off because of me. They were wondering the same thing he was: *why?*

Leave them alone. She has the memory. What had the Old One meant?

"Brooke?" Faith's green eyes met mine. "Billy has a point. The lizards did leave us alone when the big one touched you. It was like they decided something all of a sudden. Do you have any idea what's going on?"

I swallowed. I looked down at my hands—my claws.

75

"No, not really," I said miserably. "But, well, this is going to sound crazy, but when they surrounded us, it was like I could hear them talking. I could understand what they were saying. Only they weren't talking. I guess what I'm trying to say is I could understand what they were *thinking*."

Rachel's eyes widened. "But that's impossible!"

"No, it's not," said Faith eagerly. "It happens all the time on the Psychic Pals Network." Faith is a big believer in mind reading. She never misses an episode of the Psychic Pals Network, and she's always buying books that tell you how to improve your psychic abilities in ten easy steps. "Lots of people can read other people's minds. Maybe Brooke is psychic!"

"About dinosaurs?" Billy said skeptically.

"Why not?" Faith countered.

I bit my lip. I wasn't sure I wanted to be a dinosaur psychic, but what other explanation was there?

"So what did they say?" Faith demanded.

I hesitated. I knew I should just tell my friends that I'd heard the troödonts thinking that Lizard Boy had said to kill us. But somehow I didn't want to, not until I knew more about what was going on. I still didn't want to believe Lizard Boy was behind our being here. But I knew he was. I just had to figure out why.

I glanced down at my clawed hands and shivered. "They said they wanted to kill us," I told the others lamely. "But then the big one looked at me, and he said something really weird. I don't understand it . . ."

"What did he say?" Rachel prompted me.

"He said, 'Leave them alone. She has the memory.'"

"'The memory'?" Billy frowned. "That sounds like total garbage to me." He gave me a suspicious look. "You're just making all this up, aren't you, Brooke?" he added nastily. "Something's going on with you and those lizards, and you're not going to tell us what it is until it's too late!"

"Billy, don't be ridiculous," Faith snapped. "I know what the dinosaurs are talking about." She turned to me. "They're talking about your photographic memory, Brooke!" she said breathlessly.

Billy's mouth fell open. "You have a photographic memory?" he said. I could see him thinking, *So that's why Brooke does so well in school.*

"Sort of," I mumbled. "I mean, I do. But it's no big deal. My mom has a photographic memory. And so did her mom and her mom's mom. But I don't see what that has to do with a bunch of dinosaurs."

"But it must," Faith insisted. "Maybe that's why you have a psychic bond with them."

"Look, I may have a photographic memory," I protested. "But I'm not psychic!"

"Yes, you are," Rachel said. "I mean, you understood what they were thinking, didn't you?"

Billy shook his head. "There is no scientific evidence that psychic powers even exist!"

"There's no scientific evidence that people can turn into dinosaurs either," I mumbled, staring down at my clawed hands.

Faith tried to smile at me. "You haven't turned into a dinosaur, Brooke," she said gently. "You've just—"

"Got dinosaur claws and scales," I interrupted sadly.

"Which only proves strange powers do exist—at least here," Faith added with a shudder.

"And I think you've all gone nuts," Billy said angrily. "We're in a strange place surrounded by a billion hungry dinosaurs, and all you guys can do is jabber about psychic powers. We've got to get moving. We've got to find somewhere safe to hide."

We all lifted our heads. Billy was right. The silence around us suddenly seemed scary, ominous.

"Maybe they'll leave us alone now that Brooke's . . ." Rachel didn't finish her sentence, but I knew what she'd been about to say: "one of them." I felt my cheeks turn hot with shame again. Why me? Why was I the only one to turn into a disgusting half-dinosaur creature?

I bit my lip. "I don't think so," I muttered.

"Neither do I," Faith said quickly. "Billy's right. We'd better go find some shelter."

"But not with her," Billy said, pointing at me.

Faith looked at him. "What are you saying?"

"Don't you get it?" Billy replied. "She's one of them. Take her with us, and those monsters will find us for sure."

"Well, I'm not going anywhere without Brooke," Faith retorted.

"Me, either," Rachel said bravely.

Billy glared at us. "Then I'm going alone."

Just then, we heard a rumble above our heads. We all looked up. A rock came skittering down the mountainside. Maybe the wind had loosened it. But I didn't think so. I peered up into the darkness.

"Can you see anything?" Billy asked tensely.

"No, there's nothing up there," Faith replied.

But she was wrong. Maybe I *was* turning into a dinosaur. Something strange was happening to me, because I could see in the dark much better than I'd ever been able to before. And what I saw high on the mountainside was a pale face surrounded by thick, dark hair.

It was a face I knew. It was Mrs. Trowdon's son.

Chapter 16

I sucked in my breath. What was Mrs. Trowdon's son doing *here*?

Suddenly I remembered what the young troödont had said: *Kill them. That's what Lizard Boy said to do.* In a flash it came to me: Lizard Boy was Mrs. Trowdon's son. And they were somehow related to the troödonts.

A shiver ran down my spine. It was so obvious, I couldn't believe I hadn't figured it out before! The text I'd read from Dino World on Billy's laptop said that paleontologists looked to *Troödon* for clues about how dinosaurs might have evolved if they'd survived.

What if they *had* survived? What if Mrs. Trowdon and Lizard Boy were the intelligent lizard people the Dino World text talked about? That had to be the answer. I was sure of it. But I still didn't understand why Lizard Boy wanted to harm us. I also didn't understand why I could read the dinosaurs' minds, or why I had been transformed into a gruesome lizard girl when my friends all looked exactly the same.

Leave them alone. She has the memory.

I had to find out what the troödont had meant.

I peered up the mountainside. For a moment I thought Lizard Boy had vanished. But then I saw his head poke out from behind a tall, jagged rock. I had to go talk to him and find out if he was the one who had brought us here. And I had to do it fast, before Faith, Rachel, Billy, and I were torn apart by a ferocious tyrannosaur or a hungry allosaur.

Lizard Boy was the only one who could tell me what was going on. And I had a feeling the only way he would tell me anything was if I went to talk to him alone.

I turned to Faith and the others. "Go find somewhere to hide," I said hastily. "There's something I have to do—by myself."

"But, Brooke." Faith gave me a pleading look. "You can't just leave us here!"

"I have to," I replied. "You'll be okay. Billy still has his pack full of stuff. You have some food, something to drink. You'll be okay. Just go and hide, now!"

Faith took a step backward. My heart twisted in my chest. My best friend was looking at me as if she didn't know me anymore, as if I'd become some kind of alien. The worst thing was, I had! I glanced down at my clawed hands, my gross, scaly legs poking out of my old denim shorts.

"Faith, I swear I'm only doing this to help all of us," I said softly.

Faith's mouth puckered up as if she were about to cry. Then she nodded. "I know, Brooke," she croaked, biting her lip. "Just be careful, okay?"

"Yeah," Rachel echoed. "Be careful, Dino Girl."

Billy didn't say anything for a moment. I figured he was happy to be rid of me because he thought they had a better chance without me. But then he tugged at the strap of his backpack and mumbled awkwardly, "Look, I'm, uh, sorry about what I said. About not wanting you with us. I didn't really mean it. I guess I just got freaked out, you know? Anyway, good luck, Brooke. Don't do anything stupid, okay?"

"I won't," I whispered back. Then I turned and started running up the side of the volcano.

Chapter 17

I've never been a fast runner. I'm not the greatest climber in the world, either. Faith is usually a ton better at athletic stuff than I am. But climbing the prehistoric volcano that night was different. My arms and legs knew exactly what they had to do. My clawed hands were perfect for climbing rocks, and my legs had a strength they'd never had before.

I was still scared, but I was starting to feel excited, too. I felt powerful, different! I rose up the mountainside higher and higher. I swiveled my head to look down. With my improved night vision, I easily spotted Faith, Billy, and Rachel clambering over the rocks below. I hoped they would find somewhere safe to take shelter. At the same time, watching them, I felt strangely distant from them—as if I truly had become part of another species.

I turned my gaze back up the mountainside. Lizard Boy had vanished. My heart sank, but I forced myself to speed up. He was up there somewhere, and I had to find him. Otherwise, my friends and I would be trapped in Dino World forever.

I sniffed the night air. My sense of smell seemed to have grown keener, too. I could pick out so many odors—

pine needles, musty leaves, the sharp, clean scent of quick-moving streams. One thing I didn't recognize was a nasty acrid smell that made my nose prickle.

"Lizard Boy!" I called softly. "Lizard Boy, where are you? I need to talk to you!" A rock skittered down the hillside. "Lizard Boy, please come out." Another rock skittered past me. I ducked to avoid being hit. Then I glimpsed a pale face and staring yellow eyes. The face vanished behind a boulder, and I heard the faint sound of footsteps.

"Lizard Boy, wait!" I started forward, but then the acrid smell I'd noticed earlier stopped me. It was getting stronger, a smell like rancid boiled meat or old gym socks. *Phew!* I wanted to hold my nose, but I couldn't, because my hands were claws.

My teeth started to chatter again. My heart pounded faster and faster. Somewhere, very close by, there was danger!

I moved my eyes from side to side. Then I saw what was casuing the odor: the body of a huge fallen dinosaur, a diplodocus or a brachiosaur, by the look of it. The gigantic body lay sprawled over the mountainside. A pack of medium-sized dinosaurs was climbing nimbly over the beast, ripping chunks from the body with their large, curved claws. The claws looked familiar.

Suddenly, I recognized the smaller dinosaurs. They were velociraptors! Each one was only about five feet tall and weighed about one hundred and fifty pounds. But I was sure they'd killed the huge plant-eating dinosaur without any trouble.

Each velociraptor had a large, sickle-shaped claw on the second toe of each hind foot. Balancing on one foot, they could use the claw on the other to reach out and strike their prey with terrible speed. Those claws were sharper than knives.

I crouched down, paralyzed. I wouldn't stand a chance against a pack of velociraptors. My only hope was that they hadn't spotted me yet. Maybe there was time to make a getaway. But even as that thought flashed into my mind, I saw a pair of blood-red eyes staring at me over the decaying dino.

A high, keening wail filled the air. I heard the noise of scrabbling claws and slithering tails. It was the sound of a pack of velociraptors on the move. And they were coming for me!

Chapter 18

I watched the dinosaurs move toward me. Their jaws were dripping with blood, and their eyes were eager, hungry. I knew they were traveling swiftly, but everything seemed to be happening in slow motion. I had to run, but I couldn't make my arms and legs move.

The ravenous carnivores came closer. I was sure they wouldn't hesitate to rip me apart and eat me. The closest velociraptor was within striking distance now. It raised its back leg. The moonlight glittered off its long, curved, slashing claw. I heard a hiss of air as the raptor brought the claw down toward me, and I steeled myself for the blow. But nothing happened.

I stared at the creature in shock. It stood there, inches from me, perfectly motionless. It was as if the velociraptor had turned to stone. It hovered over me, claw raised, but it didn't move a muscle. The seconds ticked by.

The other velociraptors knew something was wrong. They circled around us warily, making low, angry cries. The dinosaur standing over me still didn't move. I reached up and touched its chest. It was as cold as stone.

My heart leaped into my mouth. *Had Lizard Boy somehow done that?* It was like magic. My life had been saved. Yet for some reason, I didn't feel relieved. I felt just as scared as ever. I lifted my head and peered up the mountainside. Lizard Boy was there, standing atop a tall boulder. His eyes gleamed in the moonlight, and his mouth was turned up in an evil grin. He was staring at me as if I were his worst enemy. I wondered why. And I wondered what he planned to do next.

My heart thudding, I forced myself to glance back at the other velociraptors. They were circling closer now. But none of them was coming as close as the first one had. I realized they were as frightened as I was. They couldn't understand what had happened to their leader. I held my breath as they circled me a few more times, then vanished quickly down the side of the volcano.

I turned back toward Lizard Boy. He was leaping lightly down the mountain toward me. As he came closer, a tremor of horror passed through me. From a distance he looked like a kid, but close up, it became obvious that he wasn't human. His skin was a pale, greenish color, and his yellow eyes had barely any lids and no lashes. His jaw was too thin, too pointed, to belong to a human being. And his hands didn't end in fingers but in strong, curved claws.

He looks half dinosaur, I thought, goose bumps rising on my arms. Then I caught sight of my clawed hands and shuddered. Lizard Boy and I had a lot in common.

I looked straight at him. "You're Mrs. Trowdon's son," I said slowly. "You had hands when I saw you in Fossils. But you're also Lizard Boy, right?"

The boy's sinister grin grew wider. "Right, Dino Girl. And the hands were fakes—plastic!"

I glanced back at the velociraptor still hovering over me. "How did you do that?" I whispered, gesturing at the frozen monster.

Lizard Boy laughed. "I can do lots of things," he said.

I'll bet you can, I thought to myself, gazing into his eyes. His eyes were exactly like those of the old troödont that had spoken to me. But the look in the ancient lizard's eyes had been almost soothing; the expression in Lizard Boy's eyes frightened me. He looked angry—angry enough to kill.

"You seem confused, Dino Girl. Let me help you out." He leaned toward me. "You know how the memory works, don't you, Dino Girl?" he whispered. "If you can remember something, you can see it. And if you can make yourself see it, you can make it real, make it be there, just like this stone raptor." He gestured at the frozen velociraptor and laughed again. His laughter made me feel cold all over. Besides, I had no idea what he was talking about.

Why did they all keep talking about "the memory"? What did they mean? "Well, I guess I should thank you for saving my life," I said slowly.

Lizard Boy laughed once more, a harsh, metallic sound. "Don't bother, Dino Girl," he said sharply. "I wouldn't have minded a bit seeing that velociraptor tear you to pieces. But Old One said I had to leave you alone."

There was a strange flicker deep in his eyes. "They say you have the memory, Dino Girl. What a joke!" His eyes held mine. "How did you fool him, Dino Girl?" he rasped. He stepped toward me and grabbed my arm with his clawed hand. "What are you trying to do? You'd better tell me what's going on—or else!"

Chapter 19

I tried to pull away. "I don't know what you're talking about," I gasped.

Lizard Boy's clawed fingers dug into my skin. "Yes, you do," he said. "Come on, Dino Girl, tell me. Do you have the memory or don't you?"

I hesitated a moment. Could the troödonts be talking about my photographic memory? I thought of what Lizard Boy said when I asked him how he had turned the raptor into stone: *You know how the memory works, don't you, Dino Girl? If you can remember something, you can see it. And if you can make yourself see it, you can make it real.* For some crazy reason, I thought of how I used to give my kindergarten teacher, Mrs. Murray, a monkey's head.

If you can remember something, you can see it. I looked at the stone velociraptor and I started to tremble. *Was what Lizard Boy had done the same?* Then I forced myself to keep calm. *It wasn't. It wasn't at all.* After all, I had just imagined Mrs. Murray with a monkey's head. I hadn't really turned her into a half-person, half-monkey.

"No," I whispered. "No, I don't have the memory."

"I knew it!" Lizard Boy declared grimly. His eyes burned into mine. "So what's this all about, Dino Girl?

You better tell me the whole story—now. Why are you trying to destroy us?"

My eyes widened in surprise. "'Destroy you'?" I yelped. "You're out of your mind. You're the one who's doing the destroying around here. Who brought us here, Lizard Boy? It was you, wasn't it?" I looked up at him. I could tell by the expression on his face that I'd guessed right.

"How did you do it?" I said. "Did you do something to the Dino World Web site? Tell me!"

Lizard Boy just smiled. "I already did," he replied.

Tears came into my eyes. I still didn't understand what he meant, and whatever he meant, I couldn't see how it would help my friends and me escape.

"I can't believe I ever liked you," I sobbed. "When we used to talk on Dino World, I thought you were my friend. Why did you send all these monsters after me and my friends? Why did you turn me into a disgusting lizard?"

His yellow eyes darkened a shade. "Old One gave you your claws and scales," Lizard Boy snapped. "Boy, did he make a mistake!" His eyes flashed. "So you think being a lizard is awful, do you, Dino Girl?" he asked softly. "How Old One could think a stupid human like you might have the memory is beyond me." His mouth twisted into a sneer. "Since you hate being a lizard so much, I'll do you a favor, Dino Girl. I'll change you back into your old form. Then you can go find your friends. They won't be disgusted by you then. Isn't that what you're upset about, Dino Girl? That your friends don't want to know you now that you look like a disgusting lizard!"

He took a step backward. "I'll give you your wish, Dino Girl. I'll change you back at once. Good luck. You're going to need it." He turned to go.

"Wait," I cried. If Lizard Boy left now, my friends and I would never get out of here alive. "Please wait!" I gulped. "Look, I don't think being a lizard person is so disgusting. Honest, I don't," I lied. The expression in his eyes remained as cold as ever. "Besides," I continued desperately, "I wasn't telling you the truth before. Old One was right. I *do* have the memory. Honest, I do."

"Prove it," said Lizard Boy.

"I . . . I can't," I stuttered.

He leaned toward me. "Yes, you can," he said. "You just have to put it to the test. Look at me."

I lifted my head and gazed into his yellow eyes. His brilliant yellow eyes. At first, nothing happened. Then I felt as if I were spinning around, faster, faster, as if I were being broken into a million tiny pieces. When the spinning stopped, I was in a dark place.

I smelled something burning. I was lying on something dry and scratchy: straw. I looked up and saw I was in a hayloft in an old barn. Outside, not too far away, I could hear a horse whinnying in a high, frightened voice. "Dark Star," I whispered. "Dark Star, what are they doing to you?" I didn't know how I knew the horse's name, but I did. *Dark Star, don't be afraid!*

"Set the nag on fire," said a voice. "It belongs to the dragon girl!"

I heard the horse screaming—louder, louder. "No," I started to shout. Then a hand covered my mouth, a hand that had curved claws instead of fingers.

"Child, be quiet," said a low voice.

I looked up. A woman was standing there. She had black hair and yellow eyes—and she looked just like my mother! "You must keep quiet, or they will kill us," she whispered.

"But, Mother!"

She took my hand in hers and squeezed tightly. "Child, you *must* keep quiet."

I could hear the old wooden door of the barn creaking open. The smell of smoke was stronger now. Then I heard voices and footsteps, men's footsteps. Men were storming our barn, carrying flaming torches in their hands. I flattened myself against the wall of the hayloft.

"They're hiding up there!" a voice shouted.

The men were climbing the ladder. The bright flames they were carrying hurt my eyes. Smoke choked my throat.

"There they are. Kill them!" voices were shouting.

"Mother, no!" I screamed.

But it was too late. Fire licked across the hayloft. And still the men came toward me.

Chapter 20

"**D**on't, don't hurt us. Please don't hurt us!" I screamed. Then I saw that I was on the side of the volcano again, crouched beneath a cliff of jagged lava rock. No one was around but Lizard Boy. Only now he was staring at me with a wondering look in his eyes. "Who are you?" he demanded.

I tried to answer, but the world had started spinning again. Bright lights shone around me. Once more, I felt as if I were breaking into pieces.

"Somebody help me!" I shouted.

The spinning slowed, little by little. I gasped as I felt something wet and cold on my feet. I looked down. I was standing in water up to my waist. I blinked. The water was cool and smooth and calm. The sun was shining on my back. I felt happy, peaceful. I craned my neck to look around. Green and gold lizards were splashing in the water beside me.

I laughed, a weird hooting sound that began deep in my throat. I ran to play with my brothers and sisters, splashing in the water with my clawed hands. I was perfectly happy. I traveled with my brothers and sisters across vast landscapes. We were always together under the warm sun, the bright stars. We were as one.

Then the spinning started again. Pictures flashed in front of my eyes. I saw a huge burst of light, like a star exploding above Earth. The sky darkened. Clouds covered the moon and stars. Hot ashes rained down, covering everything: trees, ferns, the giant dinosaurs that had been our food.

The creatures of Earth began to die. We crisscrossed the world, looking for food. But our warm Earth was now a world of snow and ice. We were sick and hungry. One by one, we began to die. Only a very few hung on, survived. But we all thought as one. Each of us still carried all of our brothers and sisters, past and present, in our minds, in the memories that lived inside us, memories we could bring to life when we needed to.

The images in front of me faded. For a while, I saw only blackness. Then new pictures flashed in front of my eyes, quick snapshots in the darkness. Most were pictures of me, only I was different in each one. In some I was a lizard: small and dark green with dark gold stripes. In others I was a frightened girl with greenish skin and amber eyes.

Lizard Girl, Dino Girl.

I was always running, always hiding. I had to. Wherever I landed, whatever time I found myself in, the world was full of new animals—*Homo sapiens,* human beings.

Human beings feared and hated us. They called my people and me "creatures of darkness." They called us "dragon people, serpent people." They hunted us down and killed us whenever they could. My family and I learned to fear the daylight. We learned to hide from humans' prying eyes. We learned to be creatures of the night.

Not all human beings were cruel. Some protected us and befriended us. Some even joined with us.

Darkness covered the pictures I was seeing, and the world began spinning again, faster and faster, until I felt myself losing consciousness. I was swallowed by the blackness. "Someone help!" I shouted in my mind. But no sound came out.

Some time later, I slowly opened my eyes. The sky overhead was black. The moon had vanished. I could see countless stars shining pale white, like pinpricks in dark paper. I wondered if I were dead. Then I saw a pair of yellow eyes peering down at me.

"Old One was right," Lizard Boy breathed. "You do have the memory. You're one of us, Dino Girl. You're one of us!"

Chapter 21

I gaped at him in horror. He couldn't be serious. I didn't want to be a lizard girl forever! *Maybe the whole thing was just a bad dream,* I thought. Then I stared down at my clawed hands and knew it wasn't. I let out a long, shuddering breath.

"You've got it wrong," I stammered. "My name is Brooke Atkins. I'm just a person!"

Lizard Boy's eyes flickered over me. "Impossible," he said flatly. "You have the memory!"

I frowned. "So?" I retorted crossly. "You all keep talking about my memory like it's some big deal. But it isn't. I've had a photographic memory all my life."

"What you have is more than a photographic memory."

"What *are* you talking about?" I cried.

Lizard Boy leaned toward me. "What you saw," he said.

"I didn't see anything." I tried to shut out the memory of the visions I'd seen. They were probably fakes anyway—just computer-generated hallucinations cooked up by Lizard Boy and his friends.

"Yes, you did. I know you did. We all share the memory, Dino Girl. I saw what you remembered."

"You saw nothing," I replied impatiently. "What is the memory anyway? You keep going on about it, but I don't have a clue what it is."

Lizard Boy looked at me. "The memory is our story," he answered proudly. "It is the story you lived." He leaned closer. "All of us are descended from the Old Ones. The ancient troödonts gave us the living memory of our entire history. We can call it up any time we wish."

"You mean like a photographic memory?" I whispered.

"No, not like what you human beings call a photographic memory," Lizard Boy replied scornfully. "Not a dead memory—a real, living memory. It's like a world we can go into. That's why no matter how hard you human beings hunt us or how hard you try to destroy us, we will live on. Don't you see, Dino Girl? Past and present is all the same to us."

I gasped as what he was saying sank in. "You mean you can go back in time whenever you want?" I cried.

"Not back in time—back into the memory, back into the sum of all our memories." Lizard Boy spread his arms out over the dark prehistoric landscape. "That's what this place is. This is the world made of my people's memories, the world where all my ancestors are alive forever."

"No wonder we couldn't figure out what time period this is," I said wonderingly. "It's all the time periods mixed up, right?"

Lizard Boy nodded.

My eyes moved over to the stone velociraptor. "But how did you do that?" I asked.

"The same way you used to give your kindergarten teacher the head of a monkey," Lizard Boy replied. "Only here, it can be real."

I slowly nodded. I thought I understood. He could do what I used to do when I was a kid—superimpose a picture he'd seen on top of something real. Only when I had done it, it hadn't actually happened.

I glanced at the stone raptor again. Lizard Boy had said that whatever picture he created from his memory could be real "here."

Did he mean he had this power only in the land of memory? But if that was true, how had he brought us here? I longed to ask him, but I knew he wouldn't answer. Besides, I had a feeling he had already told me. If only I could figure it out!

I threw my head back to gaze at the night sky full of stars. It looked as real, or more real, than any sky I had ever seen. "But this land of memory is real, isn't it?" I said.

"Of course it's real," replied Lizard Boy. Then he frowned. "But all of us troödonts can't stay here forever," he said sadly. "The land of memory can exist only as long as descendants of the ancient troödonts still live on Earth." A fierce light came into his eyes. "But don't worry," he added. "We will survive. We have powers you humans cannot imagine!"

"What kinds of powers?"

"For one thing, we have no need for your kind of technology. We don't need machines to communicate. We *Troödon* can read one another's minds. Our memories are our power. You humans think alone, but we *Troödon* think as one—until now anyway," he added darkly.

"What do you mean 'until now'?" I asked curiously.

Lizard Boy's mouth turned down at the corners. "None of your business, Dino Girl," he snapped.

I fell silent, remembering the visions I'd had. I'd thought they were just hallucinations created by Lizard Boy. But what if they weren't?

"So why do I have the memory?" I asked.

Lizard Boy's frown deepened. "I don't know," he said slowly. "I can't understand it. Old One told me some humans are more like us than I ever dreamed. But you shouldn't have been able to see what you saw—unless you *are* one of us."

"But I'm not," I repeated stubbornly.

Lizard Boy's eyes flashed. "I don't believe you," he hissed. "You must be *Troödon*."

Troödon, *Trowdon*—the words echoed through my brain. Lizard Boy and his mother were definitely descendants of the *Troödon*. You needed only to look at them to see that.

But I wasn't. I just couldn't be a real, live lizard person.

Then my heart skipped a beat. I thought about how the name *Trowdon* had sounded so familiar to me, like a name I had always known. In a flash I knew where I'd heard it before.

Trowdon was my great-grandmother's last name!

Suddenly I could hear my mom's voice in my head. "Your great-grandmother's maiden name was *Trowdon*," she was saying. "That's an old name, Brooke, a very old name."

I could hardly breathe. If my great-grandmother's maiden name was *Trowdon*, then I *had* to be related to the *Troödon*. I glanced up at Lizard Boy. Why didn't I look like them? Why did I look just like a regular kid? Except for my amber eyes, I didn't resemble Lizard Boy one bit.

I swallowed. My throat felt painfully dry. "I'm not like

you," I said, looking Lizard Boy in the eye. "I don't know what I am exactly, but I'm not *Troödon*. I'm just Brooke Atkins. I'm—"

"Human and *Troödon*," a voice cut in behind me.

I whirled around. Old One was there. He was resting his long head on a high rock table and staring down at both of us. My eyes widened. I'd never heard the old lizard speak aloud before. Yet his raspy, gravelly voice sounded exactly the way it had sounded in my head.

Lizard Boy's eyes narrowed. "That's impossible!"

The old troödont sighed. "Grandson, nothing in this world is impossible," he murmured. "I thought you had learned that, Lizard Boy," he added sadly.

"But she doesn't even look like one of us," Lizard Boy snarled.

"She does since she came here," Old One replied quietly. "Her *Troödon* side is emerging in the land of memory. She may not look *Troödon* to you, but I can see our blood in her." He looked at me, and his thin mouth curved up at the corners. "You do look human, Brooke, but you have our eyes," he said gently.

"Human and *Troödon*," Lizard Boy cried. "I still don't believe it."

"Why is it so hard to believe? All things are possible in the history of life," the old lizard replied calmly.

"So it's not impossible. It's still disgusting," Lizard Boy said. "How can we *Troödon* have anything in common with human beings!"

"What's so bad about human beings?" I asked hotly.

"Didn't you live the memory?" demanded Lizard Boy. "You saw how human beings have always hunted us— murdered us!"

I swallowed. The visions I had seen were real! A

strange ache filled my heart. I didn't want to believe human beings could be so cruel, but I now knew it was true. *But so could dinosaurs,* I thought, remembering the troödonts' hunt.

I cleared my throat. "I saw. But I think all animals and people are afraid of what they don't know," I said softly.

Old One looked at me; then he slowly nodded. "What she says is true, Lizard Boy," he said. "All species fear what is strange to them. Blaming the humans does no good. We are no different."

"Yes, Grandfather, so you've told me a zillion times," Lizard Boy retorted. "But you can't deny that human beings are the most vicious predators ever seen on Earth. Look at what they've done to the planet. Look at what they've done to us!"

I gulped. *Was that how other animals saw us?* I wondered. *The most vicious predators on the planet?*

"I cannot deny that you are right, my son," the old troödont said. His voice sounded tired and sorrowful. "And yet," his yellow eyes met mine, "human beings are also the most imaginative creatures our planet has ever known." The old troödont lifted his head. "In them are the best and the worst of life on Earth. Humans have intelligence, spirit. The only thing they lack is memory. That is why I told you, Lizard Boy, that we must help humans achieve greater understanding."

"What you mean, Grandfather, is that we must sit back while they destroy us," Lizard Boy declared. "And as I have told you before, my answer to that is *no*. I have chosen what I will do!"

Old One lifted his head. "You will hurt her, Grandson," he demanded sternly, "even though she has the memory, even though she is part of us?"

"If she is a human, I will kill her like the others in revenge for what her kind has done to mine," Lizard Boy replied. "But if she chooses to be one of us, I will not harm her."

His eyes met mine. "The choice is hers."

Chapter 22

I stared at Lizard Boy. "What do you mean?" I said, fear rising in my throat.

"You must choose whether you want to side with us or with the humans," Lizard Boy said.

"How can I make a choice like that?" I demanded. "I mean, I never even knew I was . . . related to you until five minutes ago!"

Lizard Boy shrugged. "You still have to choose," he said.

"I *have* to?" I shot back angrily. "Well, before I make my big choice, I have one question for you. Why did you bring me and my friends here? What did we ever do to you?"

Lizard Boy's eyes became as hard as polished stones. "You stumbled on that model," he said angrily. "I told you to forget about it. I warned you to leave it alone. But you wouldn't. All of you on Dino World just kept talking about it. The last thing I need is people snooping around the store. My mother and I would be uncovered. Once again, we would have to run and hide, all because you couldn't take *no* for an answer."

Lizard Boy's mouth twisted into an angry sneer. "You humans killed my father, my grandmother, my aunts, my uncles, and my cousins. I am tired of running from you people!"

I gazed into his furious face. To my surprise, I felt sorry for him. What Lizard Boy had gone though must have been terrible. Then I saw the cold anger in his eyes, and my heart turned to ice.

"So what are you planning to do to me and my friends?"

Lizard Boy smiled. "What do you think?" he taunted.

"Just tell me."

"I'm going to give you a chance to learn about being one of us," Lizard Boy said. "If humans had lived in the age of the dinosaurs, you would have learned what being hunted means. I don't have the power to bring all the human beings on Earth into the land of memory. But I found the power to bring you and your friends here using your oh-so-clever technology. Now you will never escape!"

There was a lump in my throat. I tried to swallow it, but it kept coming back up. I felt like bursting into tears, but I knew I had to keep Lizard Boy talking.

"How did you use our technology?" I said in a shaky voice.

Lizard Boy just grinned. "That's for me to know and you to find out," he said. "But I'll tell you this: it helped that you were all looking at the same thing."

I tried to think what he could mean. *If you can remember it, you can see it. If you can see it, you can make it real.* I swallowed. The lump in my throat felt like it was getting bigger and bigger. "But you can't keep us here forever!"

"I don't plan to keep you here forever—just until you become a dinosaur's dinner," Lizard Boy retorted.

"Please don't do this," I pleaded. "You can't do this. It's not fair!"

"Why not?"

"Because my friends have nothing to do with what people have done in the past," I cried desperately. "Like Faith, my best friend. She wouldn't hurt a fly."

Lizard Boy's eyes locked onto mine. "What about Billy Zipkin?" he asked shrewdly.

I hesitated. If Billy Zipkin knew about the lizard people, he would probably hunt them down just the way the people in my visions had. But I remembered how Billy had pulled himself together. He'd been scared, but he had wished me luck.

"Even Billy Zipkin," I said firmly. "Taking revenge on any of us because of what our ancestors did isn't fair."

"Who said nature is fair?" asked Lizard Boy. "Only you humans pretend to care about what is fair— while being the cruelest creatures ever to live on this planet. 'Fair' doesn't interest me." He flashed his crooked grin.

I didn't know what to say. I looked up toward Old One. Maybe he could persuade Lizard Boy to let us go. But to my horror, the old troödont was gone.

I turned back to Lizard Boy. "That's what you say," I cried desperately. "But Old One doesn't agree, does he? That's what you meant when you said *Troödon* had thought as one until now."

Lizard Boy's eyes flickered, but he didn't answer.

"Old One said what you're doing is wrong, didn't he? He told you using your memory like this is wrong, didn't he?" I prodded.

Lizard Boy still didn't answer.

"You're going to do it anyway, aren't you?" I said.

"It's all your fault!" Lizard Boy shouted. "If you didn't have the memory, Old One wouldn't have cared. But because you do, he forbade me to harm any of you. Now make your choice, Dino Girl. Are you human or *Troödon*?"

I gazed at the bare, rocky landscape. The night was waning. I could see light at the edge of the horizon. I wondered how long we had been here. I wondered where Faith and Billy and Rachel were now.

I couldn't believe Old One had just left like that. I wondered where he was. *Old One, come back,* I pleaded silently. *You have to help me.* I glanced around again but saw no sign of him. Lizard Boy was waiting.

"How can I choose?" I murmured.

You cannot, a voice answered in my mind. My heart leaped. It was the voice of Old One. *You are both human and* Troödon.

That's what's so awful, I replied silently. *I understand why Lizard Boy wants revenge, but I can't let him hurt my friends. Do you understand, Old One?*

I understand.

Do you want revenge on humans, too? I asked him.

I am Troödon. *I stand by my own,* he replied. *Unlike humans, we* Troödon *never turn against one another.*

Then you think Lizard Boy is right to do what he's doing? I demanded.

No. I think Lizard Boy is young. He has suffered. But— Old One's voice was little more than a whisper in my mind—*even though I think my grandson is wrong, I cannot stand against him.*

A chill came over me. *I understand,* I replied silently. *But what about me? What should I do?*

Make the right decision, Old One said.

What? I asked him silently.

"You heard him!" Lizard Boy's voice rang out through the warm night air. "Make the right decision." He smiled at me. "You have the memory, Dino Girl. Face it. You're one of us. Join with us!"

"But my friends . . ."

"Your friends stumbled into something they should have left alone," Lizard Boy said sharply.

My brain began to make sense of what he was saying. "You mean the *Coelophysis* model?" I said. "You don't understand. *I* found the model. Is that what all this is about? The model? Why were you so scared about our finding the model, Lizard Boy?"

"Can't you figure it out for yourself, Dino Girl? The *Coelophysis* isn't a model. It's from the land of memory. That's why it has feathers. In the land of memory, everything keeps evolving."

"Then why don't *Troödon* have feathers?"

Lizard Boy shrugged. "It's like Old One said, Dino Girl. Nothing is impossible in the story of life. Some descendants of *Coelophysis* became birds and grew feathers. Others, like us, kept our scales."

"I can't believe you're doing this to me and my friends just because I found the model," I said. "It isn't fair."

Lizard Boy just looked at me. "I told you, Dino Girl, life isn't always fair."

I bit my lip. "What will happen to me if I choose the other side?" I asked in a small voice.

Lizard Boy shrugged. "You'll share your friends' fate, whatever it is," he answered. "If I were you, I wouldn't do it. Share our fate instead."

I looked down at my clawed, scaly hands.

"You'd better decide now, or it will be too late," Lizard Boy said. I looked up. His mouth was curved in a cruel smile. "Your friends are almost out of time." He gestured down the mountainside.

I peered into the valley. The velociraptors were back. They were moving rapidly down the steep face of the volcano. They were moving as if in slow motion, silently, stealthily. They were hunting.

Then I saw what—who—they were stalking: Billy, Rachel, and Faith!

Chapter 23

My friends looked so defenseless. "How can you let this happen?" I asked Lizard Boy.

"It happened to us," he hissed. "You remember, don't you? You remember what being hunted felt like. Humans are much more ferocious than velociraptors ever were. At least raptors never killed one another!"

I winced as I remembered the scenes I'd lived through: the faces in the barn, people chasing me and my family, people trying to kill us wherever we went.

Make the right decision, Old One had said.

I thought of Faith, who had been my best friend forever.

"No!" I screamed at Lizard Boy. "I won't let you do this!"

I saw his face harden. "I gave you your choice," he said. "I see you've made it."

I glanced around frantically, looking for Old One. But he was nowhere to be seen. *Help me,* I called to him silently.

My child, I cannot help you. You must help yourself, I heard him say. *You must trust yourself. Trust what you feel. Trust the knowledge that lives inside you. Remember, you are part of us. You are human and not human. Remember always, my child, that for us memory is time. Time and memory are like a vast circle. In that circle nothing is lost forever. Nothing ever ends forever. The end is not forever. Remember that, Dino Girl.*

His voice faded away like a cry on the wind. I saw Lizard Boy's face looming over me. His hand reached down, and darkness closed around me like a fist.

— — —

I opened my eyes. I was standing next to Faith. I looked down at my hands. They were no longer three-fingered claws. They were just the hands of an ordinary twelve-year-old girl. Only I wasn't an ordinary twelve-year-old girl. I never had been.

"Brooke!" Faith smiled. "You're here. You're back to normal. I was afraid they had gotten you. What happened? Where have you been?"

"I . . . I . . ." I didn't know what to say, how to answer.

Faith stared at me. "Brooke, you look so scared! What's wrong?" she exclaimed.

My eyes slid across the valley to the velociraptors. The pack was moving quickly toward us.

"Ohhhh!" I heard Faith gasp.

They were coming closer. I could see their eyes glinting as they clambered over the black volcanic rock to where we were standing.

Faith turned to look at me. Her face was stark white. "Brooke, they're coming for us, aren't they?" she said hurriedly. "There's nothing we can do. This is the end, isn't it?"

I just nodded.

"We'd better stand together," Rachel said in a tearful voice.

"Yeah," Billy croaked.

The four of us moved closer together. *Maybe this is the end,* I thought, *but that doesn't mean we have to go down without a fight.*

I slid my gaze over to Billy. I noticed his backpack hanging off his shoulder. "Billy, you still have your laptop, don't you?" I hissed.

Billy nodded, his eyes glazed with terror.

"Give it to me," I ordered.

He handed the computer over. I flicked it open and turned on the switch. The graphics of the Dino World home page appeared in front of me in full color.

I looked up for a moment. The velociraptors were approaching fast. We had to slow them down somehow. Then it came to me. It was easy. I only had to do what Lizard Boy had done. I focused on the raptors. Then I tried to remember something, anything to take their place.

If you can remember it, you can see it. If you can see it, you can make it real.

I concentrated as hard as I could. I watched the bodies of the raptors coming closer, closer. I heard Faith draw in her breath sharply. Then I heard her gasp.

"What happened?" Rachel cried.

"Amazing!" Billy exclaimed.

I smiled. Where the raptors had been moments before, there were now a dozen stuffed animals. There was my old teddy bear, blown up to giant size, and the patchwork cow my mom had made for me when I was two.

"Brooke?" Faith whirled to stare at me, her eyes wide. "That's your bear. Did you do that? How?"

I was about to answer when I heard a voice in my head: *Nice try, Dino Girl, but you're not going to escape that easily.* It was Lizard Boy. I glanced around wildly, looking for him, but he was nowhere in sight. Then I looked past Faith and my heart shrank to nothing inside my chest.

The stuffed animals were gone. The raptors were back.

"Billy, shine your flashlight at them. Maybe that'll slow them down," I shouted.

With shaking fingers, Billy obeyed.

The raptors stopped for a moment, startled by the strange light. Then they came closer. Their jaws were open; their blood-red eyes fixed on us hungrily.

I could feel Faith trembling beside me. *This is what Lizard Boy meant about knowing how it feels to be hunted,* I thought dimly. I had never been so terrified in my life. Being stalked was horrible. I could understand why Lizard Boy was so full of rage. What I had seen when I traveled into the memory had made me angry, too. But my friends didn't deserve this. I couldn't let Lizard Boy harm them.

I had made the right choice. I didn't want all of us to die. Yet, there was nothing we could do against the raptors. We were helpless human beings.

Except me. I'm human, but I'm Troödon, *too.*

Lizard Boy had made me choose, but it was just as Old One had said: there was no way I could choose, because there was no way I could deny half of myself.

No matter what Lizard Boy said, I had the memory. And that meant I had power. I had already proved that to myself. I focused on the raptors—their sharp claws, their glistening teeth. I had the power to stop them. But every time I stopped them, Lizard Boy could start them up again. Besides, stopping the raptors wouldn't get us out of here.

If only I could figure out how to use my power

properly. If only I could figure out a way to get my friends back home!

I took a breath. I didn't want to destroy the lizard people. I didn't want to hurt the *Troödon* any more than they'd been hurt already. But I didn't want Lizard Boy to destroy us, either.

Make the right decision, Old One had told me. *Trust the knowledge that lives inside you.*

I screwed up my eyes. He had said something else, something about the memory being a circle, something I hadn't understood. I had a feeling that what he'd said was important.

"They're coming!" Billy screamed.

We all jumped. The raptors were nearly on top of us. We started running backward, but it was obvious to all of us that we'd never get away.

Time and memory are like a vast circle, I heard Old One say. *In that circle nothing is lost forever. Nothing ever ends forever. Remember that, Dino Girl.*

The end is not forever. What had he meant? What "end" was Old One talking about?

Then, in a flash, it came to me. He was talking about the end of the dinosaurs—the asteroid I'd seen in my vision. The asteroid that had struck Earth and killed most of the dinosaurs, all of the dinosaurs, except for a handful of my ancestors. That had been the real end of the world my friends and I were trapped in.

I stared blindly at Billy's laptop, remembering that it held a computer re-creation of the asteroid strike. I pulled up the file and watched the image appear on the screen. I remembered what Lizard Boy had told me: *If you can remember it, you can see it. If you can see it, you can make it real.*

On the small laptop, I watched a color depiction of the ancient asteroid striking Earth. I stared at the picture a moment. Then I looked up.

The raptors were closer; their scaly red and gray bodies hurtled over the lava rock toward us. The nearest one reared back on one of its hind legs. The claw at the end of its other leg sliced through the air with a whistling sound.

I closed my eyes tightly, summoning the power of the memory. I had to bring the asteroid on Billy's laptop to life within me. I had to place it in my memory. I had to remember it, see it, make it real. If I failed, my friends and I would be killed. We might be killed anyway when the asteroid struck Earth, but I had to risk it.

I closed my eyes more tightly. I seemed to see a pitch black sky; then, deep in the center of the infinity of dark space, a light appeared. It was flame orange, brighter by far than the pale light of the stars. It came closer, closer. It grew until it was the size of the sun. Soon it would hit Earth.

I opened my eyes. "You guys hold hands and get down on the ground," I ordered.

Faith stared at me blankly. "What?"

"Just do it," I said sharply.

"Hey!" Billy cried. "The raptors are running away!"

"You're right. They are!" Rachel breathed. "But why?"

"Look!" said Faith. "There's something in the sky!"

"What is it?" Billy asked.

"It's so shiny!" said Rachel, as an intense brightness filled the sky.

Then there was a deafening crash. The ground beneath our feet heaved and shook. I tried to hold on to my friends' hands, but it was hopeless. I was soaring through the air. I caught my breath. We were moving across the planet at terrific speed: the speed of light!

I swiveled my eyes around. My friends were gone. I was all alone. I was going faster and faster, so fast I was breaking into pieces.

Chapter 24

I opened my eyes. I was lying on a bare wood floor next to a big wooden wardrobe—the wardrobe in the closet at Fossils. Then I froze. In the wardrobe mirror, I could see a face—Lizard Boy's face. He was staring at me with hatred in his eyes. I saw that Faith was lying beside me. She looked as if she were fast asleep.

As I watched in terror, Lizard Boy took a step forward. Suddenly a hand clasped his shoulder, a hand with three long, clawlike fingers. It was Mrs. Trowdon.

"My son, leave them alone," she said. "Dino Girl used the memory to save herself and her friends. By all our laws, you must let them go in peace."

"But they'll tell others about us!" Lizard Boy protested. "We'll never be safe!"

Mrs. Trowdon glanced down at Faith and shook her head. "No, they won't. When the asteroid struck, the blow wiped their memories clean. Only Dino Girl can remember what happened. And she will never tell."

"How can you be sure?"

"I know," Mrs. Trowdon replied softly. "Anyway, why would she tell? She is one of us, remember? Let them go."

"Will we be able to stay here, just like always?" Lizard Boy demanded.

Mrs. Trowdon sighed. "No," she said. "Although the humans will not be able to recall what happened, in some part of their minds, they will remember something. They will be curious about us. They will want to learn more about us. We won't be safe here any longer. We must leave at once and find a new place to live."

"So we have to keep running?" Lizard Boy cried bitterly.

Mrs. Trowdon shrugged. "What else can we do?" she said. "Our time has passed, my son. We can never be safe, except in the land of memory. Now, let's go."

Lizard Boy's eyes flashed. I thought he was going to keep arguing with his mother. But then he shrugged, too. "I knew it wouldn't work," he said in a small voice. "I knew hurting them wouldn't help. Not really. I just didn't want to believe you and Old One were right."

His eyes met mine. He stared at me for a long time. "Goodbye, Dino Girl," he said at last. "If we don't meet again, take care of yourself."

Then he turned and walked out to the front of the store. Mrs. Trowdon looked at me gravely. "Do you want to buy this dress?" she asked politely, holding up the beaded snakeskin-patterned dress.

"Huh?" I said. Then I saw that Faith was awake. She rose to her feet as if in a trance. "Yeah, thanks. It's a great dress," she said. She looked at me. "Brooke, do you want the red dress, or are you going to leave it?" She pointed at the dress with the *Stegosaurus* spikes.

"I think I'll leave it," I said.

Mrs. Trowdon smiled. "Fine. I'll take this dress up front for you," she said to Faith.

Faith and I followed her to the front of the store.

"How much do I owe you?" Faith asked.

"I think ten dollars for this dress would be fair, don't you?"

"Yeah, sounds great." Faith smiled and handed Mrs. Trowdon a twenty-dollar bill. Then she leaned over and whispered to me, "I can see why some people like this store. It's dirt cheap."

I shivered. That was exactly what Faith had said when we were paying for her dress before the whole adventure started. It was as if none of it had ever happened.

I watched as Mrs. Trowdon counted out the change. "Here you are," she said, handing over a plastic bag holding Faith's dress.

"Thanks," I mumbled awkwardly. *Perhaps the whole thing didn't happen,* I thought wildly. *Perhaps I just imagined the whole thing.* Then I looked up and saw Mrs. Trowdon smiling at me.

"You're welcome," she said in her low, gravelly voice. "Please say hello to your mother for me, will you, Brooke? My son and I may be leaving, and I may not have time to say goodbye in person. But let her know that I still think about her often."

"Sure," I said. "I didn't know you knew my mom," I added.

"Oh, yes, we've known each other a very long time. We used to play together when we were children. We were almost like sisters once." Mrs. Trowdon looked at me. "I think your mother decided it was easier to forget," she added in an undertone. "Anyway, please give her the message, Brooke."

"I will," I promised.

Faith and I filed out the door.

"Weird Mrs. Trowdon really isn't so bad," Faith said

thoughtfully. "I mean, she was almost friendly today, don't you think?" Faith giggled. "Not her son, though. Did you notice how he glared at us? Maybe he hates girls or something!"

"I don't think it's that," I said. I was relieved that Faith didn't remember anything that had happened. But it also made me feel strange and lonely. I could understand why Lizard Boy had grown so angry. Keeping such a big secret would be hard. I almost wanted to believe that none of it had ever really happened, but it had. I knew it had.

For one thing, Faith had a big cut on her hand where the pterodactyl's beak had scratched her. She pointed at it and said, "Wow! I must have cut myself on something in the store. It's weird. I don't even remember doing it."

Then the bus came and we got on. Faith asked me if I wanted to spend the night. But I shook my head. I said I was feeling pretty wiped out, which was true.

When I got home, things were still strange. Although everything seemed the same, I felt different. No matter how hard I tried, I couldn't remember how it felt to be me. I kept staring at myself in the mirror, trying to decide whether I still looked like a lizard.

I played with my food at dinner, lost in thought. Finally my dad asked me if I was feeling okay. I lied and said I felt like I was getting a virus or something. Then I excused myself and started up the stairs to my room.

"Feel better, honey," Dad called. Mom said nothing, but her eyes bored into the back of my head.

Half an hour later, Mom knocked softly on my door. "Brooke, may I come in?" she said.

The door swung open before I could answer. Mom

looked at me, and I looked at her. "You seem so tired, sweetheart," she said. "Are you feeling any better?"

"Yeah," I replied. "It was sort of a busy day."

"*Mmmmm*. You went to Fossils with Faith, didn't you?" Mom asked. Her eyes met mine. I was struck by their unusual color—amber, more yellow than brown.

"Yeah. Faith bought a cool dress for the dance. I looked for a birthday present for Dad, too. But I didn't find one," I mumbled. Then I cleared my throat. "Mrs. Trowdon said to say 'hi,'" I added quickly. "I guess she's planning to move or something. She wanted to say good-bye. She said you guys used to know each other when you were kids."

"Yes." Mom nodded. "We were as close as sisters once."

Goose bumps raced up my arms. "That's just what she said."

Mom kissed me on the cheek. "Good night, Brooke."

"Wait!"

My mother's eyes found mine.

"What is it?"

"Nothing," I stammered. "It's just . . . well . . . I guess I fell asleep or something on the bus on the way back from Fossils. Anyway, I had this dream. I dreamed I went back to the time of the dinosaurs. There were these dinosaurs called *Troödon* there and—"

"How odd," my mother cut in. "I used to have similar dreams when I was a girl." She sighed softly. "They were wonderful dreams in a way, but I found it was better not to talk about them to anyone."

"Really?" I said, my brain reeling.

"Really." Mom's eyes held mine and wouldn't let go. "I found it was safer for everyone, me and all my relatives, if I learned to forget all about the dreams I had when I was young. I think you'll find the same thing. Do you understand what I'm saying, Brooke?"

I couldn't speak. In her own way, my mother had just told me she was part dinosaur!

"Please, Brooke, try to understand."

I looked away. "I understand," I said, although I really didn't.

"Good!" Mom reached out and squeezed my hand tightly. "Good night, sweetheart. You'll feel better after a good sleep. See you in the morning."

"See you," I echoed.

I had a million questions I wanted to ask her, but I didn't dare. Hadn't Mrs. Trowdon told me how Mom felt? *I think your mother decided it was easier to forget.*

Easier—or safer?

As I stretched out on my bed, I wondered if I would forget. If I *could* forget. I was relieved that everything was back to normal—in a way. But I felt sort of sorry, too. I thought about the new world I'd seen, with all the amazing dinosaurs in it. I thought about Rachel. We had become friends on our journey, but if I ever ran into her in the Dino World chat room again, she wouldn't even know who I was. But mostly I thought about Old One and Mrs. Trowdon, and especially Lizard Boy.

I hoped Lizard Boy would like his new home, wherever it was. I hoped he would get over being angry one day. As bad an enemy as he had been, in the end he had made his own kind of peace with us. *With me, anyway,* I thought, remembering that his last words to me had been, "Take care of yourself."

I wondered if I would ever see Old One or Mrs.

Trowdon or Lizard Boy again. I knew I could if I used the memory. But if I used the memory, I would never be able to forget that I wasn't entirely human. And I wasn't ready to accept that.

I closed my eyes and rolled over. But I couldn't fall asleep for a long time.

Chapter 25

"**B**illy, what is that stuff? It's disgusting!" Faith burst out beside me. I lifted my head from my desk. It was nine-thirty in the morning, and our teacher, Mrs. Zimmermann, had just told us to get out our math notebooks.

"I don't know," Billy said, wrinkling up his forehead.

"It's really gross, whatever it is," Mark Harris piped up.

I craned my neck to see. Billy was trying to pull his notebook out of his backpack, but the inside of his pack was full of clear, sticky goop. It looked like raw egg white.

"Hey!" Billy cried. He lifted up a piece of something. It was a piece of eggshell, striped green and yellow.

I caught my breath. Now I remembered seeing Billy pick up some dinosaur eggs from the cave floor and put them in his backpack.

The eggs must have broken on the way back, I told myself.

"What kind of eggs are those?" Faith demanded. She was staring at the bits of eggshell as if she could almost remember where they came from. So was Billy.

"Yeah, Billy. Did your mom give you soft-boiled ostrich eggs for lunch?" Mark Harris joked.

"No, I picked them up in . . ." Billy passed his hand over his eyes. "I don't know where they came from!" he finished weakly. "I guess someone must have stuck them in my backpack as a joke."

Faith frowned. "No, they didn't, Billy," she blurted. "Don't you remember, they're . . . " Her voice trailed off.

"They're *what*?" a bunch of kids prompted her.

"Nothing. I don't know what I was saying," Faith murmured.

"Yuk," Billy said gloomily. "This gunk's all over my math notebook." He flicked a large piece of green eggshell onto his desk.

"Gross!" everyone cried.

Mrs. Zimmermann rapped her ruler on the desk.

"Class! Class, calm down!" She looked at Billy. "Mr. Zipkin, what's going on here?"

Billy looked miserable. "I don't know. There's all this strange egg goop inside my backpack," he said.

Mrs. Zimmermann wrinkled her nose and sniffed. "Oh, dear. Well, you'd better clean it up, Billy. There are plenty of paper towels in the supply room."

"Okey-doke." Billy plodded to the back of the room. The supply room door was open a crack. He started in. Then he jumped backward. *"Arggggh!"* he screamed.

Everyone began talking at once.

"Hey, Billy, what is it?"

"Billy, are you okay?"

Mrs. Zimmermann rapped her ruler on the desk once again. "Calm down, class," she cried. She stood up and took a step toward him. "Billy," she said gently. "What's going on?"

Billy turned around. His eyes were wide. "Uhh, Mrs. Zimmermann, I think there's something in the supply room. It looked like . . . a couple of alligators."

"Alligators?" Mrs. Zimmermann's jaw dropped. "Billy, this isn't some kind of joke, is it?"

"No," Billy yelped. "I saw them. Honest!"

Mrs. Zimmermann frowned. "Maybe I should call the janitor." She headed for the classroom door. "Come on, class. I think we'd better wait out in the hall until Mr. Woolsey can make sure there's nothing dangerous in the supply room."

Everyone filed out of the classroom—everyone except me and Faith.

"Come on, Brooke." Faith tugged at my arm. "You're not seriously going to stay in here, are you?"

"Just for a second," I answered. "I want to check something out. Go ahead. I'll catch up with you."

Faith looked at me. "You're crazy, Brooke."

"Just go ahead. I'll be out there in a minute!"

Faith sighed. "You're my best friend in the whole world, Brooke Atkins. But sometimes I don't understand you at all." Then she turned and walked out of the classroom.

As soon as she was gone, I tiptoed toward the door of the supply room. I could hear noises in there—scrabbling noises, like claws tearing into paper. I pushed the door open just a crack. That's when I saw them—two lizardlike creatures, each about as big as a medium-sized dog. They had big heads, strong jaws, and lots of shiny teeth. They had short front legs and long back legs, each leg ending in a long, curved claw.

I looked into their blood-red eyes. I wanted to be wrong about what they were. But I knew I wasn't.

Billy had brought back more than he knew from the journey he couldn't even remember taking: two fertilized dinosaur eggs—eggs that had belonged to a velociraptor!

Shuddering, I wondered whether I could turn them to stone the way Lizard Boy had turned the raptor to stone in the land of memory. I stared at them and tried as hard as I could to do it. But nothing happened. The raptors just stared back at me, baring their sharp teeth. So it was true: the power of changing what was there with your mind existed only in the land of memory.

The raptors darted toward me. I jumped backward and slammed the door hard. The raptors didn't like that. I could hear their sharp claws digging at the soft wood. Before long, they would break through the door and be free.

I knew only one thing about baby raptors: they grew fast!

I took a deep breath and shut my eyes. I focused on creating a picture in my mind, a picture of Lizard Boy.

Lizard Boy, come quickly, I called silently. *I need your help!*

I thought he would never answer, but then I heard his voice inside my head. *Raptors!* he said with satisfaction. *What do you want me to do about them?*

VISIT PLANET TROLL

A super-sensational spot on the Internet
at http://www.troll.com

Check out Kids' T-Zone, a really cool place where you can...

- Play games!
- Win prizes!
- Speak your mind in the Voting Voice Box!
- Find out about the latest and greatest books and authors!
- Shop at BookWorld!
- Order books on-line!

And a UNIVERSE more of GREAT BIG FUN!

Don't miss any of these exciting books!

_____	0-8167-4279-0	#1 Meltdown Man
_____	0-8167-4280-4	#2 Lost in Dino World
_____	0-8167-4343-6	#3 Virtual Nightmare *(Sept. '97)*
_____	0-8167-4344-4	#4 Invasion of the Body Thieves *(Oct. '97)*
_____	0-8167-4427-0	#5 Double Trouble *(Nov. '97)*
_____	0-8167-4428-9	#6 Visitor from the Beyond *(Dec. '97)*

$3.95 each

Available at your favorite bookstore . . .
or use this form to order by mail.

Please send me the books I have checked above. I am enclosing $_____ (please add $2.00 for shipping and handling). Send check or money order payable to Troll Communications — no cash or C.O.D.s, please — to Troll Communications, Customer Service, 2 Lethbridge Plaza, Mahwah, NJ 07430.

Name _____

Address_____

City _____State_____ZIP _____

Age _____ Where did you buy this book? _____

Please allow approximately four weeks for delivery. Offer good in the U.S. only. Sorry, mail orders are not available to residents of Canada. Price subject to change.